MW00935225

SCARLET

AND THE MAP OF MAPS

Book One

By

H. D. OLSON

Content:

For My Three,

Ye Know Who Ye Be!

Copyright © 2021 H. D. Olson
All rights reserved.

Chapter 1

There are many people in this world who haven't a clue what they wish to do with their life. I envy them.

Walking through the cold, cobblestone streets of Devon. Feeling the wind rush into my black cloak, piercing through my white blouse, I shiver, and I wish I could be content like others, sitting at home in front of a warm fire.

But instead, I find myself headed to a tavern I've never been to, in a town I'll never see again, in search of a map I have every intention of stealing.

The moon is out, white and bright. And it leads me safely to the front door of the Cridford Inn.

The place is quiet inside. It's early in the evening and there aren't many folk to be found. I find a table in the back, with a full view of the bar and door. I'll be sure to see my target from there.

I slide behind the wooden table and across the well-worn bench. The window beside me whistles, as the wind tries to climb inside, making the half-melted candle on the table, sputter its little flame off and on.

My black pants do what they can against the cold, but my deep red vest is the only thing truly keeping me warm.

The barkeep brings me a drink before he starts preparing for the crowd to come, and a man is warming up the keys to a small wooden piano too close to the door for anyone to keep properly warm. But surely the sound of happy tunes is one of the many tools used to keep the people here long after they should have gone home.

As small crowds start to come through, loud conversations and laughter quickly follow. It seems everyone knows someone else inside. Cards come out of pockets and games begin to be played. The piano man tunes his voice and starts in on a few songs. All is as a local pub should be. All except the lack of Richard Everett, the richest man in the county, and the one with my map.

Anxiously awaiting his arrival, the groups grow bigger, and my booth looks more and more appealing to everyone around me. It doesn't help that my red hair keeps catching their attention. If it were brown, I might be ignored all together. If it were black, I could disappear into the shadows. But it's bright red, scarlet red, and why my mother named me Scarlet when I came into the world like a cannon ball on fire. I often wonder if she'd seen my green eyes first if she would have named me Grass or Leaf, but I suppose Scarlet was better than her second choice, Brick. And if I'd been born a boy, that would most certain be my name.

Sitting here, trying to control every nerve in my body, Richard Everett, the man himself, finally comes in. He isn't hard to spot. His clothes are finer. His gestures are more pronounced. And the man behind the bar turns into an adoring puppy as soon as he sees him. Running around, putting Mr. Everett's drink together, he scares a man with less money off his stool, so Mr. Everett can have the best seat and the easiest access to anything he could possibly want.

What's more, Mr. Everett doesn't even notice the special treatment. In fact, he expects it. If anything less is done, he'll take his business elsewhere, just to prove how important he and his money are. Taking a map from a man like this is going to be easy.

It isn't long before Richard Everett is one of the drunkest men in the place, and he starts to ramble off to the crowd around him.

"So, there I was, siftin' through this pile of antiques," he begins, already slurring his words, flinging his drink from side to side. "Books and papers and trinkets and such. Nothing worth buying, mind you, until I comes to this pile of old maps, you see.

Now, I loves maps, so I asks the bloke how much he wants for 'em, but it was too steep for my pockets, so I tuck the maps inside a big vase he was selling and buys that instead. He never suspected a thing. Well, I was quite happy to have my maps, yes, so I start to study 'em, see what's what. Loads of places you wouldn't believe..."

Listening to Richard Everett's exaggerated story and the detailed descriptions of the many places his maps portray, (ports in England, rivers in Ireland, and the valleys of Scotland) I ready myself for a long night. Hours pass, and finally, Everett tells his equally drunk companion, about the one map I've come to hear about. A map that leads to an unexplored island in the southern most waters of the Indian Ocean. A map that leads to secret lands and buried treasures.

For year's people have believed there is something hidden in those seas, and the possibility of so many undiscovered riches is simply too much for a young lady such as myself to resist.

How else is a pirate to begin her career if she isn't willing to steal a treasure map or two?

"Then I finds this other map," Everett continues, "different from *all* the rest, it was stuffed inside a map of Piccadilly. Just came tumbling out, see, like it was trying to get away when it got found. I bent over to pick it up, unrolled it all and such, and starts to take a good long look at it, and I says 'I have never seen this place before in my life,' that's what I says. And so I look at all my maps, all over the house, and I can't find it nowhere, so I says to my wife, 'I think this be a treasure map,' and she just laughed at me she did, but I knew there was something different about it. And there is, mate. There's all these markings and all on it and this writing I haven't ever seen before. That's why I keeps it locked up tight. I keeps it in me secretaries desk up in the study..."

But I stop listening to the rest. Now that I know where he keeps the map, all Richard Everett has to do now is leave so I can follow him home.

The bar is filling up now, and people push further inside. One man even sits across from me, burping his beer, and releasing a sour smell across the table. My view is so obscured by all the bodies, there is simply no point in staying put. If Everett tries to leave now, I'll never catch up.

Abandoning the comforts of my table, I make my way to the front of the pub until I reach the end of the bar, and run straight into a man headed in my direction. The impact is more loud than painful, but the trinket in the man's arm goes crashing to the floor.

I bend down to pick the item up for him. I don't know if he saw me coming, but I certainly did not see him in his light brown, poorly buttoned waistcoat. Looking more closely, he appears to be in his late fifties, with silver speckled dark, blond hair and a husky build. His hazel eyes resemble two almonds slanted at an angle. With thin lips, and a slightly smooshed nose, there seems to be a nicety about him as he makes apologies for the collision.

While he rambles on, I take a closer look at what he dropped. It's a cold metal box that seems to contain some type of machine inside, it feels quite strange in my hands, but what it could be used for I haven't a clue.

"May I have that back please?" the man asks.

"Did you make this yourself?" I question, my thick Irish accent making me feel out of place.

"Yes, yes, I make all of my own inventions. Well Zahn made this one first, but I've *greatly* improved it, if I do say so myself," the man says, half smiling as though he's made a brilliant joke. "But I must be on my way," he suddenly states, taking the object back, and hurrying off.

Leaving me where I stand, he disappears into the hoard of people, still clutching his object in his arms. After watching the man go, I inch closer to Everett and his listeners.

Taking a seat at the bar, I'm still able to see the strange little man as he takes a table not far off. I realize his entire focus is on Richard Everett, and I'm not sure why. After a few moments of intense staring, the strange man turns in his seat to take in the rest of the room and its surroundings, only to spot me watching him from my seat.

He seems to be taken aback, and I can see he's trying to figure out why I'm starring at him. In truth, I'm not sure why I am myself. I don't know if it's his sudden observation of Everett that's put me on guard, or my curiosity about what exactly it is he dropped a few moments ago.

"Is there something I can get you?" he yells across to me. "A drink perhaps?"

"No, lad, I'm fine."

"Are you sure? I didn't hurt you, did I?"

"No, lad, I'm fine." But even still, I find I can't stop from looking over at him and that strange object of his. What is it exactly? And why would he bring it here?

I make myself resist the urge to look at him and his machine any further and focus all of my attentions on Everett and his group. It's hard to spot him between the crowd he's gathered around himself.

When it seems safe to do so, I sneak the quickest glance back at the man across the way. He's turned all of his concentration back on Everett, and a fear begins to turn inside of me. Perhaps he desires the map as well. But he looks nothing like a pirate or a thief. What could he want with a treasure map?

He's rather old to be starting what will surely be a difficult and treacherous adventure in foreign lands where few, if any, have been before. Though I suppose all men wish for a glorious treasure to come their way before they die. Perhaps this is his last chance. If I wasn't so determined to get the map for myself, I might feel badly for the old man. But things being what they are, no one, not even a sweet looking elderly fellow, is going to stop me from finding and keeping that map for myself.

Richard Everett rises to leave a few minutes later, pushing his way through the thick crowd. I stay back when I see him rise, not wanting to spook him or catch the attention of anyone else in the room who may witness my attempts to follow Everett home. I don't need anyone here describing me to the authorities when the map goes missing. Better to keep out of sight.

Rushing through the door once it's safe, I search the streets for Richard Everett in every direction. I finally see his teetering frame, outlined by the moon, heading up the steep hill near the back of town. Following closely behind, hiding next to buildings and behind bushes, I watch after Everett.

He makes his way down a clean, well-manicured street where the fall-colored trees form an archway one can walk peacefully through. Everett stops in front of a three story, red-bricked mansion, with paned glass windows, black shutters, and a bright white door with a thick iron knocker attached. Clearly, here lives a man who's found plenty of treasure in his own way, and the loss of one little treasure map isn't going to hurt his lifestyle in the least.

I watch as Everett walks up the stone pathway to the front door and enters. My mind and conscience at peace with what's to come.

Once he's inside, I slowly advance, quiet as can be, using the shadows to keep out of sight. Despite my sly attempts, I am not the first to reach the doorway. The man from the pub is directly ahead of me. I leap forward, there in an instant, startling the man so badly I nearly destroy our cover, when he releases a small scream.

"What are you doing here?" he asks angrily.

"I could ask you the same question."

"Did you follow me?"

"I most certainly did not," I answer. "I followed Everett on my own. And when I got here, I found you."

"That still doesn't explain why you're here."

"I'm looking for something."

"So am I."

What else are we to say? I'm certainly not going to tell my secret to a complete stranger, and he doesn't seem keen to reveal anything of his own.

Impatiently I reach for the front door's handle before the man has a chance, but the knob is locked in place. Not believing I know how to turn a handle properly; he reaches for the door and does the same.

"Seriously," he states. "It's locked. He was so drunk he barely gets home, but he doesn't forget to lock the door?"

Without a word, I step away quietly, sneaking off to the back of the house. Perhaps if I can get inside, I can lock the door behind me and leave this fellow outside. Unfortunately, I see him sprinting as fast as he can after me. He finds me standing at the back entrance, failing to get inside.

"It's locked as well," I state, as he comes puffing up.

We take turns pulling and turning the handle, but it changes nothing. For being in a completely drunken state, Mr.

Everett was surprisingly conscious enough to lock all his doors, making things very difficult for either of us to get inside.

"Maybe we should create a plan to get in together," I finally say, realizing the man isn't leaving any time soon. And perhaps some help wouldn't be the worst option.

"We may as well. It's better than following each other around trying to find the same entrance. I suppose I should tell you my name since we'll be working together. It's Joshua, Joshua Brisbain."

"Scarlet."

"Scarlet what?"

"Just Scarlet."

"It's a pleasure to meet you, Scarlet."

But I say nothing in return. Clearly this Joshua Brisbain is an amateur or he'd never have given me his last name. Now I can reveal him to the authorities any time I want. Unless his name is a fake, in which case, he's just learned my name and I have nothing on him. But he doesn't seem the sort to think that far ahead. No, I should be safe. Still, it would have been better to lie about my name and keep things in my favor.

Though we now seem to be on the same side, it does not increase our immediacy into the house.

"Maybe there's another way," I muse after we've followed each other around the entire perimeter without any success.

Not wanting to break down any of the doors, I scan the rest of the house looking elsewhere for an entrance. On the second floor I see a window opened ever so slightly. Against the wall leading to the window is a trellis full of dying plants from the recently passed summer.

Mounting the trellis, I climb to the second story. The dead plants are thick with dying leaves and vines, making the ascent difficult. I bite my tongue when the branches prick my fingers and cut my palms. One little yelp could send Everett running to look out and I'd be caught in an instant. Better to keep quiet.

Reaching the window, I slowly push it further up. Only the smallest of squeaks escapes as the frames rub against each other, even though I only open it enough to squeeze through.

"Go to the back door and I'll unlock it for you," I whisper down once inside.

"All right," Joshua whispers back. "But if you don't, I'll make the most ruckus you have ever heard."

And he scurries off, leaving me impressed.

Inside the house, I cross the room I've entered and go down the stairs to unlock the back door. Though I did not wish to say anything to my new comrade about his weight, I did notice Joshua was a plump fellow who would not have been able to climb the trellis even if he had wanted to. It would have ripped away from the wall before he was halfway up.

So, deciding it would be better for the both of us if Joshua could get into the house in a much quieter manner, the back door seemed the obvious choice. And though I would have loved to leave him behind, we agreed to work together, and that's that.

I pass through most of the home before getting downstairs. Everett was not lying about his choice in décor; maps of every part of the world cover the walls. Many so brown and tattered, it's amazing they've survived so long. Once at the back door I open it to find Joshua anxiously waiting against the frame, trying to squeeze himself out of sight from any passersby.

"Come along," I whisper. "I haven't seen anyone about. We should be safe."

"Thank you very much," Joshua whispers back. "For a moment I thought you might keep me locked out."

"I stick to my word, Mr. Brisbain. Now you're free to go your way and I'll go mine."

"Right, off we go then."

I head back to the staircase. Joshua Brisbain heads for the staircase as well, climbing behind me as silently as possible. Upon the landing, I take the path to the study, certain I caught a glimpse of it when I was walking through the hallway. Joshua also takes the path to the study, nearly hugging me, he's so close.

Looking at Joshua's face, it seems he has no plans to head in another direction. He's simply waiting for me to move. Once both of us are behind the study's door, it seems we won't be parting ways.

"I have a feeling we're here for the same thing," I state, the sinking feeling of the truth settling in.

"Possibly," Joshua answers. "Let us each head toward what we want and see if we end up in the same location."

"You first."

"Fine by me," Joshua states, and he goes immediately to the desk.

"So, you're after the map as well?" I ask, coming over.

"Apparently," Joshua answers.

"I'm afraid we have a problem then."

"What's that?"

"There is only one map and I'm not leaving without it," I say, prepared for a fight.

I do not wish to hurt him, but there is no one I won't battle to gain that map.

"That won't be a problem," Joshua says with a smile, and he brings out the metal box I had helped to topple to the ground at the pub.

"I never planned to take the map in the first place," he finishes.

"What's your plan then?" I ask, curiosity getting the better of me. "Because I think we need to be getting out of here soon."

"I completely agree," Joshua responds. "Unroll the map."

Turning back toward the desk, I pull the map out from the second drawer I search and spread it across the desk's surface.

Joshua aims the front circle of his machine at the image of the map and clicks on the button located at the top.

"That should do it," he says.

"That's it? Brilliant, now I can take the real map," I answer, a little too happily. Being a pirate is going to be easier than I'd thought.

I grab the document and together we peer around the study's door to find a still empty hallway. The back staircase seems so far away in our hurry, but when we arrive at the door, we see a group of men are trying to break in. One of them is a man I saw sleeping on Mr. Everett's arm at the pub. Apparently, he and his henchmen are also planning to steal the map, but are too dim-witted to find a noiseless way of doing so.

Grabbing hold of Joshua's arm, I turn us around and head back up the stairs to find another way out of the house. As we re-enter the study, I see Mr. Everett exiting his bedroom door across the hall in his night clothes, in an attempt to see what all of the ruckus downstairs is about. As quickly as he descends, he comes rushing back up yelling to his wife, "Get the map, Emily, hurry, get the map."

"What's all the commotion down there?" she asks, tying up her robe and yawning, still sleepy eyed with the late hour.

"Thieves, they're trying to steal my map," he answers, hysteria rising in his voice.

Clearly, he too recognized the man who is now beating through his door. Hearing Richard Everett's words, it's obvious we have no time left. I turn the little lock on the door, and not a moment later the handle begins to wiggle back and forth from the other side, giving Joshua and I only a few moments more to devise a plan.

"They're stealing my map! Right now, they're stealing my map! They're everywhere," Mr. Everett yells from behind the door. "I'll catch you, you thief, I'll find you and you'll pay for stealing my map. You'll pay for this!"

Looking at the map in my hand, it's suddenly clear how much danger I'm in. If anyone finds the map in my possession, I'll never find the treasure. I'll be sent to prison. I could even be hanged. I need a clean way to escape without Everett ever knowing I was here, and the only way to do that is to leave the map behind and get out of sight.

"Mr. Brisbain," I say.

"Yes, my dear?" he asks, staring at the shaking door in horror.

"Would you be willing to give me a copy of the map from that thing of yours?"

"If you get us out of here, I'll give you as many as you like."

"Then let's go."

Folding the map back into its original state, I put it away in the exact place we found it. Exhaling loudly, I know there is no other choice but to leave it behind.

With no time to spare, I throw open the window of the study, and step onto the window's ledge. I reach out to grab hold of the tree branch some two feet away, while simultaneously swinging my leg over the tree's limb as though it were a horse's saddle.

"Mr. Brisbain, grab hold of my hand," I call back.

Shaking with fright and breathing heavily, he leans out of the window and hoists himself onto the ledge, before reaching out with both hands for my arm. Mr. Brisbain's size has not diminished in the half-hour spent at Mr. Everett's home, causing more problems than we have time to solve. And maintaining my balance sends an ache to muscles I didn't know I had.

When Joshua securely grabs hold of my hand, we go spinning in the tree, forcing me to turn completely upside down to keep from falling out. My legs lock around each other tightly. Trembling and wobbling, I steady myself as best I can before managing to lower Mr. Brisbain onto a branch directly beneath him. I right myself quickly and follow behind, lowering onto the same branch, careful not to shake us loose with the movement.

Just as the wobbling stops, we hear Mr. Everett make one more threat before the sound of his foot is clearly heard kicking the door down in his rush to grab his map and the thief.

"They're gone, they're gone!" Mr. Everett cries. "Where's my map? Where is it?"

Perching on our branch for a moment, like unwanted, oversized birds, staying as silent as we can, we hear Mr. Everett and his wife sifting through the desk. The sound of a drawer opening drifts down.

"It's here. My map...I don't understand, the door was locked. Someone had to be in here, the window is open. But they left my map..." Everett is clearly confused.

"Oh, come on, Richard, we haven't time," Mrs. Everett calls. "They're coming. They're already in the house."

Mr. Everett rushes away and goes to his wife before he has the chance to look out of the window. A few moments later, when the Everett's can no longer be heard, we free ourselves from the tree and the scene of our unfounded crime. We look around the corner of the house to see the men from the bar burst through the door. As they rush in, Joshua and I get as far away as we can.

"I'm so relieved I could cry," Joshua states, giddy with excitement, and taking gasps of air, when we come closer to town.

"Don't get comfortable yet," I say, winded myself. "We need to get completely out of sight."

We may be safer than we were a few moments ago, but that doesn't make me feel much better about how close and visible we still are.

"Then follow me," Joshua says, nearly skipping away in relief, leaving me running to keep up. He may be a round fellow, but his feet must have wings, for I can barely keep up as we leave the Everett's estate far, far behind.

Chapter 2

"So, how did they come out?" Joshua asks, peering over my shoulder to look at the photographs of the map he just developed.

"Wonderful, lad, I can see everything," I answer.

When we left the Everett's home, Joshua ran directly to his flat, a one room box, with a small bed, a giant desk, and a floor littered with papers and half assembled gadgets. It wasn't the most spacious of places, but it was cozy and warm, just like its owner, and both a little scattered.

One of the first things I noticed when we arrived, after spotting the jacket he had left behind before heading to the pub, were the numerous sketches pinned to every wall. I didn't fully understand what some of them could be, a tab that seemed to be attached to a set of teeth, or a wheel hanging from a ceiling, but Joshua was clearly an inventor of some kind.

"Did you draw all of these?" I asked.

"Oh, yes," Joshua answered, "they're just ideas that pop into my head. Drawing them out helps me to focus on other projects until I can get back to the new ones."

The man's imagination was far beyond my own. While my daydreams focused on the world around me and what I could do, or wished to do, Joshua's mind was in its own world, one I'd never thought of before, but certainly one I'd love to be in. In his head, anything seemed possible, whether I could understand it or not. One of his drawings in particular caught my eye right away. It appeared to be a machine that functioned underwater.

"And what's this one?" I asked, gently pulling the picture from the wall.

"Oh, that, I call it a 'bubble.' Never had enough money to build a prototype though."

"And it can go underwater?"

"Yes, of course, unless I build it wrong," Joshua chuckled to himself, a deep self-amused laugh, "Then it will just be a really big bath."

But I didn't find it a very funny joke, here was something I'd been looking for without even knowing it needed to be found, and when Joshua went off to develop the images of Mr. Everett's map, I tucked the sketch into my waistband.

Once the pictures were finished going through the strange chemical process Joshua tried to explain to me, we end up sitting together on the floor, looking over the photographs and the markings covering the map.

"My goodness," Joshua says, "it's such a small place to hide a treasure. I hope it's still there?"

"Aye, lad. It's there, every piece. Now we just need to get there before anyone else. Do you happen to have a map with the oceans on it?"

"Of course...somewhere," Joshua answers, looking around his home at the clutter, wondering where to search first. "Ah, right," he says to himself, as he walks over to a specific pile of papers.

Reaching for the middle of the stack, with a good yank and a backward stumble, he pulls out a wad of paper and hands the map off to me. I bend it on itself, unfolding the large sheet, to study a specific area.

"Just as I thought," I say, looking back and forth between the map in my hand and the photograph.

"What?" Joshua asks.

"It's not there. The island on our map isn't placed on this regular old map. It's probably not listed on any maps at all, that's going to make things tricky for us, because we won't know where to start."

"Oh, that's not a problem," Joshua says, smiling.

"What do you mean, lad?"

"The map—I know where it leads, I always did. I'm surprised you don't. What were you going to do with a map you can't read? It really is a good thing we stole that together, or you may never have known where you were supposed to be going."

Not amused with Joshua's comment, I stare hard at him, thinking that will make it clear I'm not happy. But he continues to look at me with his stupid grin as though he's said all he needs to say and he's the cleverest man he's ever met. I finally have to ask him outright to explain.

"So, where does it go?" I ask.

"It, no, you know what? I'm not going to tell you."

"And why not?"

"Why should I?"

I don't have an answer. Why should he tell? I certainly wouldn't if I were him.

"Maybe if we were still partners, real partners, not just out of convenience," Joshua begins, "I might be willing to tell you, but since you have your map and I have mine, it doesn't seem like we have a reason to stay allies or anything."

"What if we did?"

"Did what?"

"Kept working together. You may know where this map starts, but you may need help getting to the end. If I hadn't been there tonight at Everett's you wouldn't have your map at all."

"Possibly."

"Definitely."

Joshua isn't going to say it outright, but he most certainly would not have a copy of the map if I hadn't been there; but then again, I wouldn't either if he hadn't been around with his camera, gadget, thing.

"We seem to make a good team, you and me," he states.

"I suppose."

"Alright, then we'll join forces, and I'll start on good faith by saying that the photograph of the map in your hand takes us to the Pacific Ocean."

"That's not very specific."

"How's this for specific? There's a research vessel headed out for the Pacific Ocean leaving the day after tomorrow, down at Plymouth. They're trying to map the Venus planet as it moves across the sky."

"But we're not trying to get to Venus," I snap sarcastically.

"I know that, I know, but they have to go to Tahiti to chart it properly."

"What does that matter?"

"The map—that's where it leads, Tahiti."

"Really?" I jump off the floor, my face bright with excitement. "Why didn't you mention it sooner? We'll commandeer the boat and make them sail us to Tahiti and back! You really are brilliant."

"So brilliant, in fact, that I've been hired to work on the boat. And what do you mean by 'commandeer'?"

I ignore his question, clearly, I've gotten ahead of myself. I'll have to watch what I say in the future.

"Well, a job is fine and well for you, mate," I continue, "but how do you suppose I get aboard? It's not exactly easy for a woman to get work on a ship full of men."

"I suppose I hadn't thought of that."

"Most men don't."

"Well alright, let's think about it. I have my place on the ship, perhaps I can convince them to bring you along."

"How so?"

"I hate to suggest it, but I think it will work best if you pose as my sister."

"Sister?"

"Yes, sister."

"Don't you think that's a tad bit ridiculous?"

"I don't see why."

"Perhaps, because you're old enough to be my father."

"Father?" Joshua asks in surprise, "I should say not."

"Aye, lad, my father. I'm only fourteen."

"I don't see what that has to do with anything."

But my age did seem to surprise Joshua, even if he didn't say so, and I recognized the look he was trying *not* to give.

How could someone so young already be on her own? He was thinking. And trying to find treasure of all things? He didn't say with words. Perhaps I wasn't as fierce as he first thought. Perhaps I was simply nervous, like a little girl, and trying to figure out what to do next. But, in that moment, I also saw a little light touch Joshua. An idea seemed to have worked its way into his mind, a realization perhaps. And suddenly I felt as though I had a friend, instead of a questioner, on my side. Someone who would help, not hinder me. The feeling wasn't new, but it had been a long time since I'd felt it. I hadn't even noticed it was gone, until he wouldn't stop looking at me, in that annoying way, when you know you're stuck with someone whether you like it or not, but you also know it's probably for the best.

I wanted to punch him in the nose for that look. I wanted to warn him he didn't know what he was signing up for. But in that same moment, I also knew there would be no point. When someone's made up their mind, there's no changing it, you just hope you don't cause them to regret it.

Arguing for a half-hour more about finding a place for me on the crew, Joshua finally agrees to pose as father and daughter, though he refuses to believe anyone will accept he's old enough for the job.

"It's never going to work," he continues to repeat. "I could easily have a fourteen-year-old sister."

At such a remark, I begin to open my mouth, but shut it back up just as quickly. If he doesn't believe he's old enough to have a fourteen-year-old daughter, I'm certainly not going to convince him otherwise. Some arguments simply aren't worth having.

The hour grows late, and Joshua offers to let me stay for the night, so we can go to the docks together first thing in the morning. Though I don't wish to stay in a near-stranger's home, no matter how kind that near-stranger may be, I can't risk him leaving without me. The dependency I'm placing on this man is unsettling; I've barely begun my journey and already need so much help.

* * *

Joshua rolls over on his small bed, snoring aggressively. I'd insisted on taking the floor; felling it gave me an advantage if I suddenly needed to escape. Reaching in my waistband, I find the sketch I'd pinched earlier.

The image of the 'bubble' is difficult to see in the moonlight, but its outline is there, round and made of metal, like a cannonball with a window. Some rough bits poke out the sides of the machine, but I guess they must be there to keep the thing afloat, or for navigational purposes. It is a wonder to behold, and the real thing will be exquisite once we find the treasure and have the money to begin building. Joshua doesn't know it yet, but I have a lot of work planned for him if he's as smart as he seems.

He suddenly snores so loudly, I'm scared from my thoughts. It sounds more like a bark than a sinus condition. I quickly tuck the page back out of sight, in case he might be angry if he sees I've taken it.

Turning over to get some sleep, the deep sound of a crying whale hovers above my head as the air escapes Joshua's nostrils. I spend the rest of the night with my eyes wide open.

* * *

The dock is covered in a soft light the next morning, when we present me to the man who hired Joshua. Convincing him I'm Joshua's daughter is simple enough, but convincing him to let me board the ship is quite another matter.

"Have you lost your mind?" he snickers, "The Captain will never allow her on the ship no matter whose daughter she is."

"See?" I whisper to Joshua.

"But she has nowhere to stay when I leave," Joshua pleads.

"I'm sorry, but she cannot board this ship."

"Then you will have to do without a cook," Joshua says, trying to scare the man into consenting.

Apparently, he thinks his station is more important than it really is, and doesn't realize any man around who can boil an egg and burn a pot of tea could easily replace him.

"Fine, there are plenty of able men who can take your place," the man counters back.

I roll my eyes, knowing what the man would say before he'd said it.

"But you leave tomorrow morning," Joshua states.

"Then we'll have to look quickly, won't we?" the man snaps back.

"No, wait, wait, Josh—I mean, Father, you can't quit for me. I'm sure I can find a place to stay while you're on that ship,"

I interrupt with a strong look, telling Joshua to let the issue go before he loses his place completely.

"But, Scarlet...," Joshua begins to plead.

"Now there's a sensible girl," the man coos, "I believe that means we have a cook?"

"Yes," Joshua slowly answers, "yes, sir."

"Excellent, be here before first light. Good day."

"Good day," we answer simultaneously.

"That was my only plan, Scarlet," Joshua says, as we walk away, "I don't know how to get you on the ship now."

"There's one other way," I say.

Joshua's face falls and he stops walking. "Don't say it, Scarlet. I haven't the stomach for it. What if you get caught, or worse, I get caught, and then we'll both go to prison? We barely escaped yesterday; those blokes who came in the house after us are in jail right now. I read it in today's paper. They're sure to be hanged. I can't be hanged, Scarlet, I can't. I'm far too young."

"You don't even know what I was going to say."

"But don't I? You want to sneak onto that ship and hide until we're so far out to sea they can't possibly send you back."

"I was going to suggest killing one of the crew and disguising myself like a man before we boarded the ship tomorrow, but your plan is much better. Let's leave until night fall, and when we return, I'll find the best place to hold up," I conclude and begin to walk away from the docks.

Excited by this new idea, I leave Joshua where he stands.

"Kill a man?" Joshua whispers to himself.

"Scarlet," he calls, following after me and catching up, "you weren't serious, were you? You wouldn't kill a man to take his spot?"

"Well, perhaps not kill him, just ruff him up a bit and hide him away so he couldn't prevent us."

Joshua stops walking again and his eyes go wide with surprise.

"What is it, lad?" I ask. "You know these are the kind of things we're going to be doing if we're ever going to find where the map leads? And you had better decide right now if you can do them or not."

"I most certainly cannot. You wanted to kill a man and I thought of a way around it. And if you don't mind, that's exactly how I plan to follow that map. It only takes a second longer in thought to come up with an idea that's better than a bad one. And you would be wise to try it sometime, rather than jumping to murder and mayhem."

"Well sometimes there's no time for a second thought," I say, steaming at Joshua's remark.

Like I wanted to kill someone for no good reason. He didn't understand me at all. I was only running a plan through to its possible end, not planning outright murder.

"And sometimes," he counters, "you have to make time before doing something foolish you can't take back."

Joshua sees that my face has turned as red as my hair, as I stare down at him, but he does not waiver and stares right back. I think he's starting to realize just what type of temper he's going to have to put up with and, unfortunately, he seems more than ready for the challenge.

"Fine," I finally consent, "When we have the time, we'll do things your way, but if we're caught in a moment of action, where the only thing that will keep us alive is an instant decision with no thought about it, we do things my way. Understood?"

"That seems perfectly reasonable," Joshua admits.

I spin on my heels and walk away, Joshua following closely behind, and I can feel him smiling at his small victory, making my face redder than it's ever been.

* * *

"Scarlet, this is a crazy idea," Joshua whispers to me, as we sit huddled behind a wood pile while the sun sets behind the waters in front of us. "You can't sneak onto the ship you want to be invited on and expect them not to kill you when they find you out."

"Why not?" I ask, slightly insulted that Joshua does not think his own plan will work.

"Because it's wrong, that's why. If you get caught, not only will we go to prison, but if we ever get out, we'll never be able to go on another ship again. What if there's another research expedition in the future and they let women go as part of the team? They'll never hire you once you've been marked as a stowaway."

"We can't wait until that might happen, they may never go to the same place we need to be ever again, and especially before the treasures been found out by somebody else. This is the only way, Joshua. Now stay here and keep watch, and if anybody gets too close, give the signal. Understood?"

"Yes, but hurry up. I can't get caught out here either, you know."

"I know. I'll be as quick as I can."

I sidestep from behind the pile of wood, my bag of supplies hanging across my body, while Joshua uneasily watches me walk away. The dock is nearly empty as the day slowly fades into the colors of night. The last bits of blue and orange start to wash away from the sky as the sun melts lower. My eyes adjust to the dimming light, but the shadow cast by the side of the ship onto the dock makes it difficult to see my footing, or even a short distance ahead.

Walking slowly up the plank that was laid out for the crew from the dock to the ship, I creep up and see two men at the bow of the ship, a lit candle burning between them. From this distance they appear to be heavy set men in their thirties, darkened and leathered by numerous years spent in the sun, but right now they are laughing at each other's conversation and not on alert for any trespassers that may be coming aboard, making it a perfect situation to take advantage of.

Walking across the deck, carefully avoiding any boards that look as though they may squeak underfoot, I move forward until I find myself in front of a cabin. Slowly turning the brass handle, the door opens just enough to squeeze through, and I close it quietly behind me.

It's a small room for one of the higher-ranking crewmembers. A neat bed carved into the wall, with pillow and blankets already prepared for the occupant. A small desk to its right, a few scraps of paper carefully placed on top. Though a comfortable enough room, there is no place to hide, so I re-open the door and head in a different direction.

I'm already past the third door of an identical cabin, when a distinct dove's call comes floating to my ears. I quickly find myself on high alert. It's Joshua's signal. I'm not sure why Joshua is already whistling for me, but I do know he would not have done so unless I was really in danger of being caught. I may not know Joshua well yet, but he is already showing himself to be a very trustworthy fellow.

Carefully coming back to the front of the ship, I immediately see that the crew has grown in number. Where there were two men when I arrived, there are now a half-dozen. And though there had only been need for one candle while the sun was setting, with the absence of natural light, the men have now lit every candle the deck offers.

With so much illumination, I'm sure to be spotted before I can safely hide on the vessel, and if I'm spotted before then, my plan will never be accomplished. I need Joshua's help, and fast. I return the dove call from the most shadowed spot on the deck I can find, and Joshua springs into action at once. He leaps away from the wood pile and stands wrapped in a black cloth covering his entire body, including his face. He goes toward the base of the front of the ship and starts screaming out like a mad man,

"Oh, the ship is haunted! Oh, run, run before you all die! The spirit of Harold Jackson will kill you all! Oh please, get away, get away," and he flails his arms about and runs around in a circle to attract their attention.

It works immediately. All of the men leave their huddle to look over the ship at the crazy man running around the docks. Seeing my opportunity, I sprint for the ladder leading to the lower levels of the ship, still able to hear Joshua screaming and chanting with his distraction above.

The landing is spacious for a ship, with little rooms for some of the more important crew members, including the Captain's quarters and his private office. But I find nowhere to hide.

Going down a level lower, I come to the crews' quarters, where numerous hammocks hang from every available beam in a crazed pattern. How do the men plan to crawl inside their little lodgings with so many hanging over each other?

The massive stove is to the back, with three storage areas to the stove's left. Joshua will not have a lot of room to maneuver in such a tight space. More cabins are tucked away further down, even smaller than the ones a level up, but they are still better than the hammocks I find stuffed in a tiny and tight little nook of the same level.

Winding my way among the hanging beds and dining tables, I reach a darkly lit ladder and follow the passage down to the ship's belly. Musty and cold, I take a few unsure steps at a time, waiting for my eyes to adjust. Advancing cautiously, there are no sounds to meet my ears, this level of the ship is completely void of people, but not of livestock.

The smell of different grains mixed with fresh droppings drifts toward me before the first creature shows itself. A little goat for milking, "bahs," when it sees me coming forward.

Pushing past the animals' loosely penned little homes, I come to the main storage locations for many of the ships needed supplies, such as ropes and mops and, of course, the vast amount of food needed for such an excursion. One room in particular holds an immense quantity of fresh fruit. Something I've never heard of as part of a ship's cargo before.

With little left to explore, the options for hiding spots are becoming limited. Searching around the most promising room, I discover a small storage space with a cupboard door attached. Opening the latch and peering inside, there is little in the way of supplies being stored here. Shuffling a few things around, I create enough room for me to lie down and settle in for a very long

voyage, I only hope Joshua's distraction does not raise an alarm

and cause suspicion with anyone. If they decide to thoroughly

search the ship, I won't be able to avoid discovery. But for now,

this tiny, little space will have to be my home for as long as I can

keep it.

* * *

I sleep little while waiting for the rising sun and the

boarding of the crewmembers. The noises of the animals is

something I suppose I will have to grow used to if I ever hope to

sleep well again. Before the sun begins to peak above the water's

edge, the sounds of thumping footsteps and banging objects slowly

begins to grow, as more and more of the crew come aboard.

Awake and alert as the noises echo around me, I can hear

the men settle into their numerous hammocks, bickering over

who will have which spot, and causing more than one body to be

tossed from his bed with a loud thump upon the floor, and a jump

from me as I hold my breath every time it happens. But one of the first voices I hear is that of Joshua. He has come aboard with the initial group, quickly claiming a spot for himself and his things, and awaiting orders. But he soon falls into silence, leaving me to wonder if he is okay, until I can dimly hear his shuffling feet crossing the floor followed by an 'I'm sorry!' before he falls into silence again.

Hours pass before everything settles into order, a few men do come to the lowest part of the ship, but they do not stay long or search too deeply within, and shortly after their departure, the ship sets sail. Settling back into my little hole, beginning to feel the sway of the ship as it rocks my body with a swooshing motion, I find I'm too happy to be bothered by it. Happy to still be hidden and on my way. Happy my new partner is safely lodged upstairs. And happy the first danger of being caught has passed.

With a smile on my face, I slowly fall off to sleep, my mind at ease with the knowledge that when I wake, we will be far out to sea and even closer to my treasure.

Chapter 3

Knock, knock. "Scarlet," Joshua whispers, as he gently taps the door.

It's the earliest of morning, when only a few of the deck hands are awake and roaming the ship.

Slowly the door opens and I see Joshua crouched on the other side with a plate of food in his hand.

"Breakfast," he says.

"Thank you, lad," I quietly answer, my voice still sleepy, "here's the plate from yesterday." A dish of bones and crumbs is exchanged for today's eggs and bread.

"How are things up there?" I ask, the words feel funny in my mouth since I've been able to speak so little since our arrival.

"Same as they've been the last few weeks," Joshua answers.

Everyday Joshua brings me my meals, and being the cook makes keeping small portions off to the side very easy for him, but sneaking them down to see me in the middle of the day is not. Though we've been out at sea for quite some time, there still remains a great risk every time Joshua comes around. The earliest of mornings are the only moments when I can expect to see him for more than a few minutes; otherwise, I'm trapped in my little hole for most of the day, silent, trying to keep from being caught by the crew.

"How about down here? Are you holding up?" Joshua asks.

"Fine, lad, I've been sleeping mostly. The only time I have to worry is if the men slip down here to get supplies, and of course when they tend the animals, otherwise, I'm usually alone."

"Good, good, I worry when I see someone headed for the stairs. Captain says it will rain tonight, so you should be safe to come up for a while."

I beam at the news. Taking every advantage I can to climb out of hiding and work my arms and legs seems the only thing I can look forward to. And rainy nights are the best, because the harder it rains the harder it is for anyone to see who, or what, I really am. The night sky only adds to the advantage. Even when the men have come close up to me, they've never realized I'm not supposed to be there. I simply answer, "Aye, aye," to anyone who speaks to me and escape back downstairs when they leave.

"Finally, my backs been aching for a stroll," I say, trying to stretch unsuccessfully.

"I'll let you know when it's safe," Joshua states.

"Thank you, lad."

"I'd best be off, see you tonight."

And Joshua leaves with the empty plate, while I eat my morning meal.

The foul odor from the animals keeps most of the crew away. Only those assigned the station come down and they leave as soon as their work is over. To give myself a break and to keep the men away from my hideout, I spend as much of each day that I can cleaning the stalls and brushing the animals down, even feeding them from the supplies. The first few weeks I was uncertain as to what to do for each creature, but watching the unwitting crew from the little slits behind my door, I learned everything there is to caring for a ship's livestock.

Once breakfast is finished, I climb from my hovel and begin work, no one the wiser for how everything is always getting done before a sailor has even shown up. Most just shrug their shoulders and leave; a few even sneak in a nap before they go. But there is a pride in doing work that needs finishing, and in a small way, I'm earning my place on the ship whether anyone knows it or not.

"Top of the morning to you, old girl," I whisper to Gladys, the goat, patting her down, "and how are we this fine morning?...Is that so? Well, you certainly look as though you have your sea legs about you. I, on the other hand, am as wobbly as a dog on ice. Did you sleep well?...That's good. Oh me? Well, I slept as well as can be expected, seeing as there's not much else to do."

After sharing morning pleasantries with Gladys, next come the pigs, and there's even time leftover to play as quietly as possible with the two greyhounds who wonder about the ship as they please. Oh, what I would give to be one of them. It doesn't seem to matter if any of the animals on board are girls, just me, but I finish off my morning routine, waiting for Joshua's arrival and the all clear to come on deck once the drops start dropping.

* * *

Late into the night, Joshua comes as promised. But I knew he'd be arriving soon, with the rain pounding on the sides of the ship, rocking it harshly back and forth, salt water seeping through every crack and chasm it can find. If he didn't show up when he did, I was going to leave without him.

Banging on the door, unworried that anyone will hear him through the roar of the sea, Joshua signals me. Crawling forward, Joshua's water-soaked body is standing before me.

"I'm not sure you want to come up tonight, Scarlet," he yells above the sound of the pour, "There are more men than usual on deck. I guess we're in a pretty strong storm."

"I don't care, Joshua," I have to yell back, "I can't stay in here a moment longer. Everything aches and smells."

"Then you better wrap up as well as you can so no one will see you."

I throw on a big jacket I took from one of the sailors who left it behind after his nap with the chickens, and wrap a scarf around my head to hide my hair and face, before we climb the stairs to the deck to see the rush of commotion, as men run every which way tying down the sails, securing the riggings, and trying not to drown in the onslaught of rain and waves that crash over

their weary bodies.

"It's worse than I thought," I scream toward Joshua, so I

can be heard.

"Perhaps you should go back," he yells even louder

himself.

"Maybe I can help."

"I don't think you should push it, Scarlet, we've got a long

way ahead of us and we've been lucky you haven't been found out

yet."

"I can't stay down there forever, Joshua," and I go off to

pull down a runaway rope, before it releases a sail that would have

snapped in two.

"Thank you, lad," a voice yells out beside me, before he

too grabs hold of the rope and helps me tie it down. "That was a

close one, aye lad? Captain would have had me head if you

hadn't grabbed hold of that there rope."

"No problem, sir," I reply and scurry off before the man can get a really good look at me.

"Hey, where you headed?" the man calls across the deck, "We be needing help at the bow. Make your way over; I'll be there soon as this rope stops fighting orders."

My shoulders cringe together in dread. Joshua was right; I was pushing my luck walking about the deck so openly.

"Aye, aye," I shout behind me, and make my way to the bow of the ship, Joshua following behind and turning very pale.

"I told you this would happen," he hisses beside me.

He and I secure more ropes with the rest of the crew, Joshua standing in front of me, trying to block as much of my face from view as possible.

The man I'd helped earlier, only a few feet behind me.

"I know, lad, I'm sorry," I hiss toward Joshua's back. "But what was I to do?"

"Stay away," Joshua replies.

I exhale loudly. I know he's right, but I also know he's not the one who's been sitting in a hole for weeks on end unable to do anything simply because I'm a girl on a man's ship.

"How's it coming down there?" It's the man from before, calling over to us.

"Fine, sir, just fine," Joshua yells back.

The man is in his forties, thin from years of hard work on numerous ships, sun burnt and blond and glassy eyed. He's clearly taking a notice of me whether he means to or not, with a continuous glance toward me and Joshua every chance he gets, unsure of what he is trying to find, but clearly suspicious of something.

"You need to leave, that man you helped keeps looking at us," Joshua whispers.

"Tell me when he's not watching and I'll make a run for it," I say.

"Alright...now," Joshua commands. I dash across the deck and down the stairs as fast as I can.

Safely below, I yank off my wet disguise and pace the room outside my hiding place, thinking there must be something I can do, some way I can gain welcome on this ship without being tossed overboard when they find me.

While anxiously running the situation through my mind, a slow creaking on the stairs makes me stop. I dive for the door to my little hole and scurry inside, careful to close it as quietly as possible, bringing my soaked clothes with me, and hopefully every trace of my presence as well.

Peering through a thin crack in the wooden planks, I can see the man from above deck come around the corner and gaze over the room. I hold my breath and stare at him, willing him to leave with all my might. When he sees no one in sight, he heads back up the stairs, and I shut my eyes tight in relief.

"Joshua will never let me out of here now," I think bitterly, as I curl my wet body into a tight ball, horrified at what this could now mean. I may never be able to leave this hole again,

not until we're safely in Tahiti, and even that may not go as planned.

It seems even the smallest of hopes is pointless, and now my one relief, walking about the ship unnoticed in the rain, is gone too. The saltwater from my eyes mixes with the saltwater already covering my skin, and runs unchecked across my cheeks. The bitterness of this situation seeping in.

It had all seemed so easy back in England. Just climb on board and wait it out. But the waiting is more than I can stand, and perhaps the hardest thing I've ever done.

Eventually I begin to drift off to sleep, the rocking of the ship more soothing than disruptive. I just need to get through the night, and perhaps things will seem better when the morning comes around. I let myself wander off to dreams and the comforts they bring. Knowing, at least for the moment, I'm safe where I lay. Until the morning comes, it's best to sleep away the sadness and the fear, and hope Joshua isn't too angry with me when he comes.

Chapter 4

Another month passes, and Joshua continues to bring me food and water. But after nearly being caught, he never attempts to invite me on deck again, claiming it to be too dangerous. Instead, I creep up on my own in the dead of night, hiding among the shadows, and letting the dark wind blow across my face. It may not be the warmth of the sun I crave too desperately, or the group I had hoped to join and work with, but it is better than the cold wet of rain, or the endless smell of hay mixed with aging wood I'm always surrounded by. I've nearly been caught a half-dozen times, but what Joshua doesn't know can't possibly worry him.

"I'm happy to see you staying with our decision to hide down here for the remainder of the trip," Joshua says one day, my supper in his hand.

"Right," I answer, quickly taking the bowl without further comment.

"Right," Joshua repeats, "Well I best be off. Your last dish please."

"Yes, here you are. I, well, Joshua, I've been thinking, perhaps...perhaps I could come out of hiding, go to the Captain and explain everything..."

"Absolutely not," Joshua answers, horrified, "There is no way you're going to anyone and telling them anything. You'll be thrown off the ship and then they'll throw me off for getting you on. No, Scarlet, I must insist, you're going to stay right here out of sight."

"I can't keep hiding down here, Joshua, not for forever. Even if we get to the island, we still have to get back. That's months and months of hiding, if not longer."

"So?"

"So, I can't do it, I need to be up there, working, learning. How else am I to navigate a ship of my own someday if I can't even learn how this one works?"

"I...I don't know, Scarlet, but I can't...I can't lose you if something goes wrong. We've just started and I don't even know how to begin once we reach the island, I'll never find my way to the treasure if I'm alone."

I look at Joshua and see the worry on his face.

"And what do you mean by 'a ship of your own?' I thought we were in this together," he continues with a smile.

I can only smirk back. The loneliness inside me must be showing itself more freely. I know there is little he can do to change it, but the guilt still seems heavy on him. If only I were free to come up like Joshua.

"I didn't mean anything by it," I continue, "about my own ship I mean, I just thought...well, I just thought you might not want to travel around with a—pirate," I answer uncomfortably.

Joshua smiles down at me.

"I always had a suspicion that might be your goal," he snickers.

But I should have known he'd figure it out. How else can a woman, even a young one, stuck in this time, even attempt all the grand plans I have floating around in my head? I would either have to be an eccentric and powerful woman with loads of money, which he knows I am not, or a pirate. And since pirates have few rules in regard to membership, it seemed the best fit.

"Really?" I say, a genuine smile showing itself now, one I haven't shown since we first arrived, "I thought I might scare you off if I ever said anything."

"Well, you wanted to kill a man less than twenty-four hours after meeting each other. It was either pirate or murderer," Joshua answers, "Though I suppose one could argue they're not that different. But Scarlet, pirate or not, it isn't safe for you to walk around up there. It's barely safe for me."

"Alright, how about this, I'll stay down here if you promise to teach me everything you learn up there?"

"That's a wonderful idea, Scarlet," Joshua says, the fear leaving his face, "I should have suggested it myself, and I promise to come down here more often to teach you about the ship and to keep you company, but I better go for now, it's already been a long while."

"Right," I say, actually handing over my empty plate this time and closing the door to the hiding place. It might be a small change we've come up with, but I'll take almost anything to lessen the boredom.

I stay hidden for yet another month, only coming out as needed to visit and care for the animals, but Joshua does what he promised and finds more time to come see me and provide the best instructions that he can. The ship continues sailing for a total of three months before reaching its first official destination, the Rio de Janeiro, without incident.

"How's it going up there?" I ask one morning. The ship is the most stationary it's ever been, and I can feel the itch to go ashore whether I'm allowed to or not.

"Fine, just fine," Joshua answers, "The Captain's a real gentleman. Can't say the same for the officers, but that's how it goes."

"And the crew?"

"Oh, the crew is wonderful, their manners could do with a little polishing up, but other than that they're a wonderful lot."

"That's good to hear," I reply, "How long until we reach the Cape?"

"Not long now I suppose."

"Wonderful."

And so our conversations go as we journey forward. I'm not always able to contain the bitterness inside at my trapped circumstance, always longing to be with the crew, seeing what they see, doing what they do, even though Joshua tries all he can to ease my discomfort. Anything he can find that won't be missed, he brings for my entertainment, whether it be stories of the day or small objects used for different tasks, ropes with varying knots in them being one of my favorites and easiest to smuggle down. They're like small puzzle I have to put back together once I untangle them.

When the ship finally reaches Cape Horn, it brings with it a sudden shift in the winds and a terrible storm. For two days the Captain fights against the worst weather we've yet faced. The clouds roll in on the crew, and I can hear the skies anger through thunderous yells, while the lightning flashes bright light through every slit. The sea is so disturbed that it laps up and against the ship without ceasing. Even though I'm hidden deep within, I can feel every jostle and shake the ship is exposed to. I can hear every man above, running from one part of the ship to the other, desperately trying to outrun the storm, and despite every effort, it will not let them rest. The crew cannot seem to push against the onslaught and round the Cape.

I rock back and forth in my hovel, water seeping through the cracks and leaving me as dilapidated as if I were above deck. The animals moan outside my door, wet and as miserable as myself. The water is simply everywhere, and nothing is dry, and, like the animals, there is nothing I can do about it.

I only hope Joshua is still safe.

Suddenly, the pounding of heavy footsteps bangs against the stairs as a crewman comes down into the room. I do hope it is Joshua, but it is more likely someone sent to check on the poor creatures, scared and unknowing in their little pens. I listen in complete silence as they make their way through the room, when suddenly my little door is jerked open.

I gasp with surprise, it is the man who'd been watching me those few months ago, when I'd stayed on deck for too long.

"Come along, miss," he yells at me, "or you'll drown with the rats."

He reaches in and jerks me to my feet and out of the hole.

"But how did you...?"

"That fellow of yours ain't too sharp," the man answers. "He's been sneaking down here every other minute and it ain't been without notice. Now come along."

"But I can't, they can't know I'm here, they'll kill me."

"It won't matter what they do if the storm kills you first. It's going to kill us all at this rate. A man was swallowed by the sea right before I came to get you and he wasn't the first, which means we're short-handed and desperate. So, if you want to liv, I suggest you come with me and take his place or it will be the end of everyone on this ship."

I say nothing, as I follow the man up the stairs. Some of the crew I pass by pause in their steps to look at me before my companion snaps them back to their senses and barks for them to get back to work.

"Aye, aye," is their only answer, but I can feel them watching me as I continue forward. The rain crashes against our faces, taking our breath away and chilling us anew as we find the spot on deck where we're most needed.

"Grab hold of this line," the man yells, as he tosses me the end.

I dash over and hold on with both hands. The reality of being up here, open and visible, is too surreal to be true. I can't even think clearly. My shoulders are up to my ears, partly to block the cold, but mostly in a lame attempt to hide myself.

"Now, PULL!" he screams at me, waking me from my false invisibility, and we pull.

"PULL!" and we pull the line again.

"PULL!" until the rope is as tight as we can manage.

"Now come along," the man calls, and he takes me by the arm and to the next station. Over and over I follow him to every job that needs completing, trying to beat the storm and save the ship with every effort.

"Now over here," the man yells, and at last I run into Joshua. His eyes go wide at seeing me. I let out a deeply held breath and my eyes water over, my face as red as my hair.

"Scar...Scarlet?" he asks.

"No time for that now," my companion orders.

And the three of us snap our mouths closed and start in on the next sail, but the entire time I can feel Joshua's eyes piercing through me. If I wasn't so wet, I'd be covered in tears. I've ruined everything for the both of us. If we survive the storm, we're both dead anyway, and all because I couldn't stay put and leave Joshua alone. Why did I have to jeopardize him too and beg him to risk notice by seeing me more often? At least one of us should have made it to the end, to see where the picture of the treasure map led.

We say nothing to each other while the storm rages. No one does. No one can sleep or eat during the ceaseless battle. When the waves finally settle on the second day, everyone is beyond exhausted. Those that can move, crawl to their beds, while the rest simply collapse on the deck as the newly rising sun begins to dry their weary, wet bodies.

My hands bleed with the countless blisters covering my palms and I can barely breathe from all the salt water that has trapped itself in my lungs. Joshua is close by, coughing and wheezing. He received the worst of the last row; a giant wave came crashing down on him and another crew member while they were working and now, he lies nearly motionless, coughing up a belly full of salt water.

As I watch my friend, I see the Captain clearly for the first time, walking through the collapsed bodies on deck, his coat dripping bits of water as he goes by. He does not say a word or bark a command. There is a strength in his silence, making him appear taller than he really is. Though a Captain now, his body still shows the molding of being a sailor himself for many years. Strong arms and a strong back, his eyes distant and far-off, as if he's already ahead of the ship, safely landed at his destination, and waiting for the rest of his body to catch up.

A shame comes over me, for lying there, for being too tired to move. I roll to my side, the pain coming back anew, but I'm able to push myself up off the floor. Certainly, I can find the strength to check the riggings and make sure all is secure? It is my duty to these men and to my Captain no matter what may happen to me when the storm settles, and I will not let them down, not when the end is before us. I may not be a part of their crew, but it will not be because of my own short comings. If they don't want me, it will be because of their own thoughts on the matter, not because I can't hold my own.

I cross from one side of the ship to the other. The entire time I can feel the Captain watching me, and I begin to wish I'd stayed where I was on the floor, instead of making my presence more felt and more known, until I'm finally joined by one man after another and disappear into the crowd.

Silent and weary, we finish our work as a unit, the battle won, the storm lifting.

Chapter 5

The dark clouds which consumed us, vanish by next day, and the blue skies cover up all trace of the danger we just experienced. But the damp railings and floor hold the truth in their waterlogged boards and no one onboard can forget what we've survived or those who have not.

When the sun pierces through the clouds, and all signs of danger seem to have past, a small ceremony is held in honor of the fallen men. But Joshua and I are not in attendance. We weren't welcome. Instead, we're huddled together between the hanging hammocks and the dripping clothes recently washed by the sea, awaiting our fate.

"I can't believe you, Scarlet," Joshua chastises, "What are we to do now?"

"I don't know," I answer, "but I couldn't very well die in that hole, now could I? I had to do something to help those men, to help *you*. I didn't know if you were dead or alive, Joshua."

"But now they all know and we can't undo it. And I don't understand how that man found out about you anyway?"

"He watched you coming up and down with my food each day."

"So now I suppose it's all my fault?"

"It's not your fault, Joshua, it's mine. I was bound to be found out sooner or later."

"Yes, you were," says a booming voice behind me.

"Captain," I whisper, turning to face the visitor.

"It is a rare day when I am not aware of what is happening on this ship, Miss...?"

"Scarlet," I quietly answer.

"Miss Scarlet. And I'll have you know there is even fewer a chance of me not knowing *who* is on my ship."

"I...."

"Never mind that, Miss Scarlet. Do you know what I could do to you—what I should do to you? A trespasser for months, a stowaway eating our food, drinking our water. I could have you hanged when we get back to shore."

"You can't...," Joshua says, leaping from his hammock.

"And the man who helped her, easily hung right beside her," the Captain continues, as Joshua sits back down, "but rather than wait, why not have you two walk the plank? I'd be perfectly within my rights to do so."

"Please, sir, leave Joshua out of this, it was all my idea; he only helped me because I threatened to kill him if he didn't," I state.

"I'm well aware of Mr. Brisbain's role in your being here, Miss Scarlet, and I don't care for liars. He is just as much to blame for your being here as yourself." And he slowly begins to pace the narrow lodgings.

Joshua and I sit there frozen. There is no escaping. Where can one run on a ship in the middle of the ocean?

"I have an idea," the Captain says, stopping, "Lieutenant, come down here please."

A tall, thin man comes trotting down the ladder; the same man Joshua and I had met at port months ago.

"You," he hisses, anger spreading across his face in recognition.

"Ah, I see you've met," the Captain says.

"Yes, Captain, she was trying to get aboard ship before we left the docks."

"And it appears she has succeeded."

"I didn't allow..."

"Yes, Lieutenant, very well, apparently your answer was not acceptable to Miss Scarlet, for here she is. The question now is what to do with her."

The Lieutenant smiles at the idea.

"Bring her and Mr. Brisbain above deck," the Captain orders.

He turns and walks ahead of us, while the Lieutenant happily grabs hold of my and Joshua's arms and shoves us forward. Skittering across the floor in resistance, we find ourselves above deck, with the sun shining blindingly across our faces. The storm has relinquished its hold and given way to a bright and glorious day, showing no sign of the previous turmoil. It is as though the crews struggles and worries had been imagined. But, unfortunately, not for me and Joshua, standing next to each other awaiting a decision that will most certainly be worse than the storm we survived.

"As I am sure you have all noticed by now," the Captain begins, "we have an uninvited guest among us."

The men on deck stop what they're doing to listen to the Captain speak. Many stare, and a few gasp, but most give only a quick glance before waiting for the Captain to continue.

"This is Miss Scarlet," he says, "Apparently a good friend of our cook, Mr. Brisbain."

"A stowaway, Captain?" one of the men yells across the deck.

"I'm afraid so," he answers. "That is why I am coming to you all now, to decide the fate of Miss Scarlet, and Mr. Brisbain, her accomplice. Now, I am of one mind as to the course we should take, but she has defrauded not only myself but the rest of the crew as well, and I am obliged to hear what your view is on the subject."

The Lieutenant smiles widely at these words, while holding me in place. Seeing the grin, I give a hard yank on my arm, causing him to trip on his own footing. Smiling at the effect, I accidentally snicker in satisfaction, only to be grasped more tightly when the Lieutenant recovers.

"I know what we should do with these miscreants," the Lieutenant states, his fingers bruising me through my shirt.

"I thought you might," the Captain says, without warmth. "Does anyone else have an opinion?"

"I do, sir, if you'll hear it," a man says from the middle of the deck. It is the same man who dragged me from my hiding place in the storm. "I be hearing the words stowaway and miscreant, and that may be all well and true, but this lady hear is also part of the crew, at least she were the last few nights. I was beside her during the storm and there ain't man nor boy aboard this ship worked as hard as she did. If it weren't for her help, I dare say we wouldn't be discussing throwing her overboard, because we'd all be floating in the ocean right beside her.

Now I don't believe what she did be right, but she never hurt a soul on this ship, and if it be a matter of where to keep her, well there be enough empty hammocks and spare food now, bless the souls who passed last night to give them. Captain, I speak only for myself, but I cannot bear to see another soul tossed to the merciless ocean, screaming for its life, and not able to do a thing to help it."

A long silence follows the man's statement, as each member of the crew remembers the pain and loss of the last few days.

"Do any others feel as this man?" the Captain finally asks.

"Aye, Captain," an aimless voice answers.

"Aye," follows another.

"Aye, Captain."

"Aye," "Aye," "Aye," a dozen voices ring out.

The only one who does not follow suit is the Lieutenant, still clutching my and Joshua's arms, determined to keep us prisoners for as long as possible, and gasping with anger at every man's answer to keep us alive and well.

"I believe that settles matters then" the Captain states. "And I must say you have been the very men I expected you to be. Release your hold, Lieutenant. I don't know where you ever expected them to go anyway.

It has been a long night, and morning has shown little relief, let those who can be spared be off to bed, the rest do what you must. And Mr. Brisbain, I believe we are well past the breakfast hour, if you wouldn't mind putting something together?"

"What, sir? Oh, no, no, I wouldn't mind at all," Joshua says, the realization that he and I are not being thrown out into the ocean forcing a broad smile to his face and stirring him from his waking nightmare. "I'll whip something up right away, sir, right away. Come along, Scarlet."

I quietly follow Joshua across the deck and past the men who have decided to spare my life. I want to thank each one of them, to show my appreciation, but their minds are on different tasks, and they seem to care little that I'm even still there.

Some look at me as I pass, but no one says a word, so I remain silent. Perhaps I can show my 'thanks' later on, when my happiness at still being alive does not conflict with the sadness of the death of their friends.

Chapter 6

Joshua leads me into the sailor's mess, where the kitchen, dining tables, and sleeping quarters are all located together, and the biggest pile of clutter I have ever seen, with dishes scattered about, and clothes and food scraps littering the floor. The big black stove, where Joshua now stands, with almost no room for his frame to squeeze in and actually cook, is already ablaze and awaiting his orders. It reminds me very much of Joshua's home back in England, all cramped and filled with endless things.

"There you are, Mr. Brisbain," a voice calls from behind, making me jump, "I couldn't find you, so I went ahead and started with the potatoes."

"Ah, that a boy, Joseph, and thank you. I wasn't entirely sure I'd be making breakfast, or anything else after today, but at least I knew you would be here to carry on in my absence," Joshua says, patting this Joseph on the back with warmth.

While Joshua is speaking, he fails to realize that Joseph knows nothing of me or the situation which has just occurred on deck, and as he finishes his statement, he finally sees the confusion on Joseph's face as he stares openmouthed at me.

"Oh, right! Joseph, this is Scarlet; Scarlet, Joseph," he says, as though that clears everything up.

Joseph remains silent.

"Pleasure to meet you, Joseph," I say, still surprised myself to be just hearing of Joseph and meeting him in the same moment.

"But you're, you're a girl," Joseph spats, starring wide eyed at me.

"Correct," I answer, a little bitterness in my voice. Didn't I just reveal all of this to the crew five minutes ago?

Looking at the young man, with his stupid brown eyes, and mess of red hair, it's no wonder Joshua never mentioned him before. He's so pale he looks as though he were the one living in a hole for the last few months and not me. Still, I can't help but eye him with suspicion. Why hasn't Joshua mentioned him before? It seems quite clear they've been working together for a while now, and yet, not a word about him.

"Yes, Joseph, this is the friend I was telling you about in England," Joshua continues.

"But you never said your friend was a girl...or that she was here," Joseph says.

"You're quite right, but I simply couldn't under the circumstances. You understand of course, don't you, Joseph?"

"I...I suppose so," he answers.

"Excellent," Joshua continues on, as though none of it even matters, "I'm sure we'll all get along swimmingly. Well, perhaps I shouldn't say 'swimmingly.' Scarlet and I did almost take a swim of sorts a little while ago, but enough of that. Joseph, the Captain wishes breakfast to be served immediately, and that's exactly what we'll do. Scarlet, help Joseph bring up the rest of the supplies, and I will get these beautiful potatoes further along."

I turn to leave, happy for a distracting task, but Joseph waivers a moment before leading me to the stores in the very bottom of the ship, not knowing I'm already well acquainted with the ship's lower decks.

Once there, he does not speak a word. He grabs supplies, piles them into my arms, and proceeds to fill his own. Looking at him while he grabs what we need, he's average in height at best, a stocky boy with strong arms. Clearly, he's been doing something on this ship to produce such a sturdy frame, but I ask him no questions as he leads the way back to Joshua.

"Excellent, excellent," Joshua states at our return. "And Scarlet, the Captain wishes to see you. Don't look worried my dear, he seemed in a rather decent mood, considering."

I look at Joseph one last time before leaving, but he does not return the glance. Following Joshua's directions, I end up directly in front of the Captain's "Great Cabin," the door ajar as I approach.

"Come in," the Captain calls. Papers, maps, and charts are scattered atop his desk. Holding a quill in one hand, he jots down some pressing matter before looking up. "If you plan to stay on this ship there will be things you need to attend to," he begins.

"Of course, Captain," I state, my voice quieter than I intended.

"You can start by cleaning the officers' cabins each day."

"Yes, Captain," a little louder.

"That includes this room here and the officers' mess."

"Yes, Captain."

"And I'm certain your friend, Mr. Brisbain, will be in need of assistance on given occasions."

"Yes, Captain."

He looks hard at me before making his next statement.

"My Lieutenant tells me you posed as Mr. Brisbain's daughter the first time you attempted to board this ship, is that true?"

"Yes, Captain. We figured if your lieutenant thought we were related we stood a better chance of getting me aboard, being female and all."

"I see, well it was a clever attempt none the less. I think you'll find his cabin to be the most difficult to clean unfortunately. That is if he lets you enter it at all."

"I see, Captain."

"I certainly hope you do. You've put me in a rather difficult spot, Miss Scarlet. One I won't soon forget. The men will be quite unsettled for a while, I'm afraid."

"Yes, Captain," I whisper uncomfortably, and all my fears of being a girl among unhappy men come back.

"That will be all for now, you are dismissed."

And I turn to leave.

"One thing more, Miss Scarlet," I pause and turn again to hear what the Captain wishes to say, "I do not expect these men to show you favoritism, in fact, I insist they do not. But extreme behavior in a negative fashion will not be tolerated, and I hope you will come to me if need be."

"Yes, Captain. Thank you, Captain."

"Good, that is all I have to say."

I take a deep breath and return to Joshua, finding him right where I left him, just finishing the morning's meal. The many hammocks surrounding the kitchen are filled with weary men, and many heads pop over the side, breathing in the smells of hot food, and snatching a look at their new comrade.

"I don't know, Scarlet, I'm not happy about you being out in the open now," Joshua says, seeing all the curious eyes.

"It'll wear off, Joshua, just give it some time. They won't even notice me soon enough."

"I certainly hope so. What did the Captain want?"

"Just giving me my orders is all. I'm to clean the officers' cabins primarily and help you when I can."

"Good, you can help now. These plates need to be taken to the private cabins. Joseph will help you and show you the way."

* * *

The private cabins are split between the lower deck, where we were now, and the after fall, where the Captain's quarters are located. The privacy of the rooms makes them much nicer and cleaner than anywhere the sailors spend their time. For one thing, their beds are not hanging in the air, swaying back and forth.

"About time," the Lieutenant says, when I unknowingly arrive at his room. If I'd had a clue it was his I would have made Joseph bring in the meal.

I quickly hand him the plate of food and begin to leave.

"Aren't you forgetting something?" the Lieutenant calls, forcing me to stop in my retreat.

"What might that be?" I ask.

Turning swiftly around to face him, our bodies are only inches apart, as the Lieutenant looks down at me from his few inches of advantage.

"The cabins? They need cleaning. Or haven't you been informed? Perhaps you intend to ignore what you've been told and do what you like instead, since you're rather good at that already?"

My fingers twitch slightly in anger. Here's a man I'd fight on the spot if we were back in England, but as it is, I've barely survived this day, and there's Joshua to think about. I can't cause him anymore trouble.

"You coming, Scarlet?" Joseph calls behind me. I'd forgotten he was still there and his voice startles me. "Joshua will be wanting to see you before you get started on your other chores."

He must have been watching the interaction, because he sounds determined to drag me away.

"Right, I'm coming," I say to Joseph, breathing deeply and pushing away the anger, forcing myself to leave before I do something stupid.

"See what I'm talking about?" the Lieutenant continues, "you can't even answer a superior when you're spoken to."

At the remark, I take another deep breath and turn to answer the Lieutenant's question with as much respect as I can muster.

"So sorry, sir, I'll be back shortly to clean the rooms," I say.

"Much better," the Lieutenant states, glaring at me, "now leave my sight."

Happy to escape without having to say another word, I walk on with Joseph beside me. He won't look at me, but he was clearly trying to help, and I'm, yet again, silently thankful. Controlling my temper is going to be harder than I'd thought.

When we return to the kitchen, I help Joshua for a few moments more as he finishes preparing meals for the sailors themselves. Normally they roll up their hammocks and eat at the tables, but their exhaustion is still deep and nearly all would rather eat their meals in bed.

I may not have fought in the storm for as long as they did, but I envy their rest. My hiding away has left me out of shape, and I feel weary to the bone. But I'm alive and walking about the ship in the light. I'll just have to muddle through till day is done.

"Why did you never tell me about Joseph?" I finally get to ask Joshua, while handing him a plate to fill.

"No reason really. Why? Do you not like him?"

"No, I don't know him, but we've been here for quite a while, and every time I asked you about the crew, you never once told me about your new friend."

"I guess...I guess I thought you might be jealous."

"Jealous?"

"Yes, because he was up here and helping me and you were hiding downstairs unable to do anything."

"I see."

"I wasn't trying to keep him a secret, I just didn't know how you would react and it was already difficult enough for you to keep yourself locked away all this time. I do hope it doesn't change anything. He's a nice boy and he'll come around. You just have to get to know him is all and I'm sure you'll both get along."

"I'm sure you're right," I answer, smiling a little to ease Joshua's worry. He's probably right, I would have been jealous, and I couldn't be sure what that jealousy would have made me do.

Leaving the cook's mess, I head to the Captain's quarters, but he's still studying in his great cabin. Not wishing to disturb him anymore today, I make plans to return later on, and head to his personal cabin instead. I sort through the mess as best I can. The room is so small, with a bed taking up nearly all of the space, cleaning it is easy.

The next two cabins are even smaller and though half of the men are extremely messy, leaving dirty clothes on every surface or littering their rooms with an assortment of papers, the rooms are so little that even the messiest of them does not take long to clean properly. I'm able to return in a few hours to find Joshua on deck just finishing the last bits of his own breakfast, before he hands over a plate he's saved for me.

"You should have seen the sailors, Scarlet," Joshua begins, as we sit and look over the rails at the light blue ocean, while the waves gently splash against the sides of the ship. "Animals, all of them, their plates were empty before you even left the room."

"That's a ship's crew for you," I say, looking at my own quickly emptied plate and the amusement on Joshua's face as though he were reflecting on a new species.

"How do you know so much about ships and their crews?" he suddenly asks.

"Well... I don't know much," I answer, trying to hide my face from Joshua as much as I can, but he's standing so close, the attempt is pointless. "You see," I continue, since he will not stop staring at me, "I only know what I've read and heard about here and there. The truth is, Joshua, I've never sailed in my life; it was really only a dream—but that's going to change right quick. We're on this ship now, see, and I can learn all I need to know. So don't you fret, I'm going to learn everything I can on this voyage."

"Oh, I'm not worried. You're going to be a great sailor, Scarlet, just think about all we're going to learn on this trip. In fact, I think I'm actually going to like it here, especially since I don't have to worry about you any longer."

"Good, because I can't wait to get into the grit of it all," I answer. "I believe I underestimated you, Mr. Brisbain. I didn't think you would last this long, not with me anyhow."

"Nonsense, Scarlet, we must work together and learn together. I'll make a deal with you. I'll do everything in my power to help you become a pirate, if that's what you truly wish, and in return you help me fulfill my dream of becoming a proper inventor."

"Alright, Mr. Brisbain, you've a deal."

"Fabulous, and please give Joseph a chance. I'm certain you won't regret it."

I'm not sure this is the case, but if Joshua likes him, then I'll have to at least try to find something about the boy I can stand.

"Fine, I'll do my best," I answer, as the ship clips through the light blue waves of the early morning sea, and I smell the salty air.

A freedom I did not think I would ever feel comes over me, and for a moment, I'm not bound by what I am, only by the possibilities of what I can be.

Chapter 7

Joshua and I continue with our everyday chores while aboard the ship, at each day's passing becoming better and better at completing our tasks. And I quickly learn all of the ins and outs of a well-ordered ship.

I watch the sailors around me in awe. Liam, the man who found me and forced me to come out of hiding, is the most impressive. Though years spent on various decks have weakened his knees and bent his back, he is still stronger than most of the men, and with a much better temper. He keeps most of them in line, while simultaneously gaining their respect. I've no idea how I'll ever do this with my own crew, but if I can find a way to carry out even a little of the example Liam sets, I know I'll be heading in the right direction.

"So how do you like our little troupe?" Liam asks me one day when things are quiet and not much work needs doing.

"They're wonderful when they can bother to look at me," I answer.

Liam laughs, "That's because you haven't been properly introduced."

"What do you mean? We've been working together for weeks, not to mention surviving a massive storm."

"Those things only showed them you can pull your own weight, and they like you for it, but now they need to respect you, see you as one of their own."

"And how can we do that?"

"Have you ever heard of 'Captain's Mistress'?"

I smile broadly at the name, "Have you ever lost to a girl?"

* * *

Despite its name, "Captain's Mistress" is nothing more than a simple marble game, so named because of our Captain's obsession. Not a man aboard believes the Captain loves it less than his own wife, and few dare to play against him. But among themselves it's a nightly ritual; one I've only had the option of watching from afar.

I learned the game as a little girl in pubs surrounding the docks, where it was called "Four in a Row." More than once, my talent to see different patterns and varying outcomes was the only reason I was able to eat that day. Almost no man ever turned down the chance to beat a little girl who wished to throw her money away, even when she had won the last ten rounds.

As Liam leads the way to the lower deck, the rules of the game come back to my memory. Four marbles have to align at any angle. So long as the opponent's marbles do not block the path, the first to accomplish the task wins. Inside the room, a group of men have already formed in the furthest corner away from the ladder. Their backs face us, covering any site of the board while a candle flickers shadows across the wall and melts onto the large barrel they use for a table.

"How many turns, Roberto?" Liam asks the man leaning on the back wall of the ship.

"Fourteen," the sailor, Roberto, answers.

It's clear he's been sitting there a while, a large pile of coins next to his right hand showing his winnings.

"I'm next," Liam calls.

Two minutes later, the man across from Roberto lets out a groan when Roberto's marble falls into place and he wins his fifteenth straight game.

"Come along, Liam, and hand over your money," Roberto calls.

Liam takes his seat and smacks two coins upon the lid.

"A double bet," Roberto says. "If you really want to lose twice as much as you need to, that's fine by me."

"One coins for me and ones for the girl," Liam says, aiming a thumb at me as I stand awkwardly behind him. Roberto is one of the sailors who dislikes me most, and though I've been itching to play a round ever since I found out the game was being played, it's almost always Roberto at the table, who looks straight through me every time I attempt to come up and play.

And now I'm hiding behind Liam, afraid to show my face, like a coward.

"What girl? That's not a girl, that's a stowaway, and if it weren't for that blasted storm that killed so many of our kind, we would have thrown her to the fishes."

"But as it is, we be needing her. Seeing as we're so shorthanded. Which makes her one of us, wouldn't you say?" Liam states. "But if you're afraid of losing your money, we'll be on our way." And Liam reaches down for the two coins, as he rises from his seat.

Roberto grabs Liam's hand to stop him, and Liam slowly sits back down.

"Alright, I'll play the girl, but for both coins. Agreed?" Roberto says.

"Agreed," and Liam rises to let me sit.

As I silently switch places with Liam, Roberto resets the game. The wooden board stands upright about a foot across and forms the lid to a wooden box. The Columns for the wooden marbles are carved through and align right to left with an opening at the top to slide the marbles into. Roberto reaches for the wood slab at the board's base and pulls it to his right, releasing the wooden marbles that clank loudly inside the box.

"I play white," Roberto states. "Captain's color and all."

"Is that right," I say, finding my voice. I look Roberto over, pushing forty, he still looks young. If it weren't for his constant scowl, he wouldn't even look as mean as he acts. He's tall and thin, and his brown skin glows in the candle light between the tattoos covering his arms. But there's something about him that reminds me of the men I've been playing against since I was only five years old. There's a confidence he carries with him, a confidence he shouldn't have, because no one has ever shown him how misplaced it is.

Roberto goes first, as the reigning champion, taking the middle slot. The marble smacks the board Roberto replaced at the base, vibrating against the landing. I follow by placing a brown marble to the far right, making the same thunking noise at the bottom. Roberto places his second on top of his first, forcing me to block to keep him from building up to three. Roberto counters with a white to the left of his first marble, trying to build a four set from the side. Rather than block a third I go to the right of his first marble to keep him from burning the candle in both directions.

Slightly taken aback, Roberto pauses before the next move, a third marble in a row on the left, I block his fourth and he has to create a new strategy. The game continues with each new marble adding another layer. Not until the board is more than three-fourths full, does Roberto deal his death ball. A white marble placed perfectly to guarantee he not only can win with his next move, but the next three. In his excitement he fails to realize, that by placing his marble in that slot, the very spot that looks so beautiful in his narrow mind, he himself let free the one place where I can position my fourth marble and win the game.

I release the brown marble from my hand until it smacks against the one beneath it, no one seaming to realize that I've just won.

"And now I'll teach you how to win a proper game," Roberto sneers in his excitement. The other men are giddy with anticipation, starring at Roberto's hand, which still holds the white marble in mid-air.

"I think that's already been done," Liam says from his dark corner. When the game began, he shrank away into the dark recesses of the ship, seeming uninterested in the outcome, and even now he lay aloof, nearly asleep, with his eyes barely open.

"What are you talking about old man?" Roberto asks roughly.

"Take a look at the board, you aged eel, and maybe you'll see what your pride wouldn't let you."

"It's...it's not possible, how? You cheated," Roberto hisses.

"She didn't do a blessed thing but beat you at a game you've been practicing at all night."

"I—I'm just tired, I guess. Been playing too long," Roberto says, backing down, rubbing his neck with his left hand to distract himself, but still angry. He stares across at me unbelieving.

"Sure, lad," I say, "It's been a long day."

"Right," Roberto says and he rises from the table.

"Aren't you forgetting something?" Liam calls, still lying back.

And Roberto pulls two coins from his pile and tosses them toward me before leaving.

"Have a nice night, Roberto," Liam says, as the man walks by him.

"You as well, Liam," Roberto states, pouting slightly, despite all of his winnings jingling in his leather pouch.

"Well, who's next, boys?" I call, too happy with winning to be afraid any longer.

The men all look at each other before answering.

"I'll have a go," one man calls.

I turn to see who has accepted the challenge and see Joseph standing behind me.

"Really, lad? You want to part with your money so soon?" I ask.

"We'll see about that," Joseph answers, taking the empty spot, smiling broadly, and bouncing his seat closer to the board.

Since meeting the boy, I will admit, I've grown to like Joseph's boyish charm. But his youthful tendencies are also the reason for much of my frustration. Dropping pots and pans and dishes is a daily expectation, but his constant distractions are the most aggravating of his characteristics. Joseph watches every single bird we come across with giddy joy, and the fish, as they jump from the water, has caused him to drop more than one dirty plate into the ocean. But his worst distracter of all is Joshua. Every invention, notion, or rambling thought Joshua comes up with causes the both of them to pause in whatever they are doing until every rough bit about the idea is polished away, no matter how burnt breakfast, lunch, and dinner are in the end. I've had to come behind the pair repeatedly to lower the flame, just so the crew would be able to eat their meal without losing any more of their teeth.

Joseph's joy soon subsides when he loses the game to me rather quickly, by concentrating most of his energy on the candle flickering beside us. But he's soon followed by half-a-dozen men who also wish to lose their wages. Liam left over an hour ago, but Joshua finds his way down to the fun and watches happily as each wooden marble is dropped in its place upon the board. My pile grows larger, as the men who lose keep demanding a rematch, something I'm more than willing to oblige.

"And there is the final blow," I tease a younger sailor who wished to play.

"I certainly hope not. I've yet to have a turn," a man calls from behind me.

"Then come over, my lad," I answer, inviting him with a gesture of the hand. But my sight is distracted by the many coins stacked by my side. "Though this be the last round. The hour is late." *And I want to count my money.*

The room grows silent when the man enters, and even as I speak, the crew dare not make a sound. The man takes his seat and I stare, mouth agape, as the Captain looks at me.

"Captain, sir, I'm sorry, I didn't realize it was you," I say, all flustered.

"Not to worry," the Captain states, "I admit, it is on rare occasion that I venture down this passage; but when Roberto Gomez is complaining above deck about losing to our resident stowaway at a game I most thoroughly enjoy, well I must admit my curiosity bettered me.

Shall we restart the game?"

"Of course, Captain."

"I love this part," he states, pulling the little plank that releases the balls. "I am white, of course."

"Of course."

And he places his marble to the far right.

"Wonderful move," I comment, having used the same as an opener many times myself.

"I hope you're not trying to flatter me, Miss Scarlet. I assure you I show no mercy when at battle."

"Certainly not, Captain. For I show no mercy myself."

"So, you do not plan to let me win?"

"On the contrary, sir. I plan to destroy you."

"Finally. A true opponent." And the Captain smiles broadly before the onslaught begins.

The game is quick and fast. For every attack there is a counter attack. Not a marble is placed that is not rapidly hindered by the challenger. The crowd around us gathers in tightly, the heat from sweat and heavy breathing is oppressive in this tight corner of the crowded ship. Layer upon layer of marble is built, with neither of us able to build beyond two in a row, until the final two slots are left.

"If both turns were mine, I would beat you," the Captain comments, as he twirls his last marble between his fingers.

"As would I," I say, holding my last marble as well.

The Captain places his marble in the slot, lining three in a row. I follow suit and place mine in the final slot, giving me three in a row. With no empty spaces left on the board, the game is complete, and the Captain and I come to a draw.

"I must say, that is the strongest, most enjoyable game I have played in a very long time," the Captain says, rising from his seat. "I do hope we can play again."

"It would be a pleasure, sir," I answer, rising as well.

"Goodnight, Miss Scarlet." And he turns to leave.

"Goodnight, Captain."

Joshua congratulates me on a very well-played game, he was watching throughout with droopy, half-closed eyes.

"Oh, Scarlet," Joshua says through a yawn, leaning slightly against me for support. "That was a wonderful match. Simply splendid, but I really must be off to bed. I feel so sleepy, for some reason."

"Yes, Joshua. Goodnight, lad." And I pat the hand resting on my shoulder.

The crew quickly departs, to go slump into their hammocks and begin snoring, along with Joshua, who snores loudest of all. The hour is very late, but a few of the lanterns are still in use, making it easy to spot Liam sitting in a corner on the opposite side of the room.

"It appears you were right," I quietly call, as I come closer to him.

"Of course I was," Liam answers.

"I have to thank you, lad. I don't know how I would have continued on if it weren't for your help."

"You would have found a way. But don't be forgetting, there are still those who mark a person from the start and never let them forget it."

"I won't. Here you are," and I toss two coins in his direction.

"What's this?"

"The buy in money."

"Ah, I thought you might have forgotten."

"I never forget a kindness."

"I suppose there's no chance of you splitting your winnings to show just how grateful you are?"

"Not a chance."

"That a girl!"

Chapter 8

As the ship sails forward, Joshua and I are continuously set to work, whether it be swabbing the deck or gathering ropes or hoisting the sails. The list of tasks never seems to diminish, and never seems to change.

The seas remain calm, with light, clear waters meeting us in the early morning light, and deep, royal blues greeting us in the evening. When we sail closer to land, seagulls fly overhead to great us. But every day the same chores are carried out in the same setting.

"I am getting quite bored with peeling onions, Scarlet," Joshua comments one day in the kitchen. "Not to mention the endless tears. My eyes are on fire."

"Aye, lad," I reply, as I help him with the mean vegetable. "I had no idea the ocean could be so...the same. But no worries, when we get our own ship, we won't be doing the chores. Just think. You can spend your whole day sitting in your cabin building anything you can think of. And I can steer the ship with the guide of my compass, while barking orders at our unruly crew, who will of course be planning mutiny on a daily basis. But when I pull my sword out and threaten them all with the plank, they'll go crawling around doing whatever I tell them to. Won't it be grand?"

"Ummm...," Joshua replies, staring at me, as I demonstrate my most threatening sword pose with the help of a peeling knife. "I suppose the building part will be pleasant," he carefully states, "But why exactly are we hiring an 'unruly crew'?"

"Because, we can't expect an honest crew to help us steal treasures, now can we? And besides, a group of thieves will be more fun," I answer.

"I suppose, but do they all have to be so—ruthless?"

"No lad. Just half of them, is all. They can't all be untrustworthy. No, we'll hire a handful of truly good men, the kind that will help us no matter what and stand by our side when the wicked are trying to kill us all in our sleep. Perhaps some of the men from this ship will come with us after our voyage."

"I don't know about all of this, Scarlet. It's starting to sound *very* dangerous and on our own boat mind you. Aren't the places we're going to scary enough? I don't want to sleep with a pistol under my pillow while we're at sea as well."

"Oh, don't be so difficult. What do you think a pirate's ship is like? A holiday? It will be as dangerous as it needs to be, nothing more. And if you like, you can put a knife under your pillow instead."

"Wonderful...Ah, Joseph, magnificent timing, Scarlet was just telling me how she plans to get us all killed by our own crew."

"Brilliant," Joseph answers, joining us in our work.

"Joshua," I hiss, surprised at Joshua making such an open statement in front of Joseph.

"Oh, don't worry, Scarlet. Joseph is well aware of our little endeavor."

"What?"

"Well, I thought it only right to inform him of the situation since he'll be joining us."

"Joining us how, exactly?" I ask, anger barely hidden in my words.

"On your journey, miss," Joseph answers, "I told Joshua here I'd be happy to follow him to his own ship whenever he gains one."

"It will be *my* ship."

"That's fine too, miss, so long as you be needing my help, I'll be there."

"Fabulous," I answer sarcastically.

"I knew you'd see things my way, Scarlet. You said yourself we could hire men from this ship and we had one all along," Joshua chimes in. "Now all we need is to buy that dastardly boat and we'll be on our way."

But I'm not happy with Joshua's audacious behavior toward Joseph. Telling him our secrets and promising him a job aboard our ship. My ship even! A rather bold decision. How much has Joshua shared with this practical stranger? I might like Joseph more than I first thought possible, but Joshua is giving away all of our plans, and without my consent. It's simply infuriating. If Joseph gets between me and Joshua any more than he has, I might find myself treading water while the two of them go off to find the treasure themselves. I need to find out if Joshua's said anything to him about the map, and if he's uttered so much as one word, he's going to find himself in the drink instead.

* * *

When the ship successfully rounds the cape, we reload with supplies: food, water, and wood. As the crew goes back and forth to fill the ship's hauls, the team of scientists set out to take samples and study the land. Joshua is so enthused by the prospect of exploring the yet undocumented plants and wild life, that he begs to be a part of the expedition team, and is granted pass by the Captain to join the scientists. I remain behind to help with the loading, which delays my interrogation of Joshua.

Since Liam introduced me to the rest of the crew, and I won most of their money at "Captain's Mistress," nearly all of the men treat me as an equal on board the ship. Especially when it comes to physical labor and exhausting work. But despite the difficulties, this is one of the happiest moments in my life, and I can't help but smile broadly as I take hold of another orange crate and stuff it inside.

While waiting for Joshua to return, I go below deck to visit with the animals I once spent all of my time with. They still remember me when I approach, especially the goat, Gladys.

"I won't tell anyone about this if you won't," I whisper to Gladys, lifting the latch of the gate and letting the goat follow me around the deserted level.

A ship is a terrible place for animals. They cannot go up ladders or wander around; and they almost never see the sun. They spend day after day kept in their designated locations throughout the entire voyage, and their sea legs are never very good. Gladys topples over more than once before I lead her back to her pen.

"Sorry, girl, I guess animals and the ocean don't mix," I say, petting the little head as Gladys looks up at me.

Its many hours before Joshua returns with the remainder of the crew, but in his absence a strong wind pushes itself into the area, swirling snow and cold air throughout the ship, brushing against the crews' faces as it howls with cold breath. The group was not prepared for snow, believing the weather would only be sunny and warm this far south, and there is nothing to keep the frost from clinging to our thinly clothed frames. So, it is with little surprise that we all become very ill, very quickly.

Joshua is so sick with cold that he can't even leave his hammock, and all of the cooking falls on me and Joseph as he rests and recovers. Even though we too are keeping runny noses at bay with everyone else, and wishing the constantly rocking ship would stand still for just one moment.

"Thank you, Scarlet," Joshua says through a stuffy nose. "I was getting a bit chill."

"Of course, lad," I answer, placing my own blanket across him. "I don't know why you had to go and get yourself sick. You shouldn't have been out there. You're not even a scientist."

"I completely resent that comment," Joshua says, his red and sleepy eyes glaring at me, while his lower lip begins to pout. "I may not be a man of scientific discovery, but I do wish to understand how things work—plants included. It would amaze you how much can be invented by simply understanding the way a plant or animal functions, both internally and externally, and then applying those same basic principles to material objects."

"I don't care about a silly invention if it means you getting sick over it."

Joshua is silent for a moment, unable to find an argument against the remark, but he soon explains that his inventions are "not silly" and dismisses the remainder of my comment before falling fast asleep.

Joshua does soon recover, but two of the scientists are not as lucky and die from the terrible illness while at sea, changing the mood on the ship dramatically from one of hard work and determination, to one of sadness and fear. Another terrible storm, or even a battle with natives, is more likely and desired then simply becoming ill and perishing in one's bed.

The remains of the two scientists are wrapped in cloth and weighed down before being placed in the water and sent out to sea.

Despite the shock, few cry over the event, except Joshua, who feels so grateful and also so terribly guilty to not be one of the men, that he weeps uncontrollably. But everyone else is silent. This is their way of life. There is never a promise of return when one goes out into the unknown and endless sea.

While still above deck, the Captain leans over the railings to watch the bodies sink beneath the surface and out of sight before turning to the men.

"I know this is not what any of us expected," he begins, his head slightly bowed as he addresses the crew. "But the sea cares not who crosses her path. We are on a dangerous voyage and have been lucky thus far to not have lost more men. We will move on from this tragedy and we will continue on in our quest. Do not lose heart. We have far to travel before we meet our end, and this will not be the only setback we will face. But we are strong and we are capable, and, God willing, we will all come out of this alive and together. So, man your posts, men. Our journey awaits."

The crew is slow to move at first, but as the Captain's speech seeps into their minds, the mood shifts slightly for the better, and in a few days' time things are yet again in working order.

The breeze is good, the sails are strong, and the crew is moving forward alongside their fearless Captain.

And Joshua, Joseph, and I are back in the kitchen peeling and chopping and cooking away. Suddenly, the repetition of the sea and the chores of the ship are a comfort, when it seems we've already lost so much. Knowing what is expected of us, brings with it a peace of mind. Perhaps if we stay together, we will make it through to the end of this journey without another loss.

Chapter 9

Two months pass before the ship encounters any further activity. The crew carrying on from day to day until we finally gain site of the coast of Tahiti.

Pulling into the cove and disembarking, the crew begins to scatter themselves throughout the area, discovering all the place has to offer, most notably the solid floor under their feet.

"This is the ideal time to set our plan into motion," I say to Joshua, as we watch how freely the groups head out in every direction.

With so few people to see our actions, I don't want to waste a moment of this rare freedom. Living in a small space with so many men for so many months has put me in a constant state of display. Now that the men have other surroundings to occupy their time and sight, I'm not as distinctive as usual, and I rather like it that way.

"Yes, this would be a wonderful time. How shall we start?" Joshua asks.

"We need to grab our things off the ship, including the food and water."

Getting what we need is an easy task, and luckily, Joshua has taught Joseph all of the skills required to keep the kitchen going in his absence.

"I'll be happy to take over for you, Mr. Brisbain," Joseph says, when asked to cook the meals and keep our departure a secret from the crew.

"Thank you, Joseph, you don't know how much this means to me and Scarlet," Joshua answers, grabbing his belongings and beginning to follow me up the ladder.

"Yes, Joseph, thank you," I say, running up the steps in double time. "Now, come along, Joshua."

"You will be handsomely rewarded upon our return," Joshua states.

"He'll what?" I call from the top, certain of what I've just heard, but unbelieving.

"Well he'll certainly deserve something, won't he?" Joshua yells hotly behind me.

I rush back down, "How much have you told him?" I whisper, loudly.

"About what?" Joshua asks, almost falling backward with my sudden appearance right beside his ear.

"About any of it," I hiss back.

"I only mentioned why we would be needing to leave the boat."

"You what?"

"Well I had to tell him something, didn't I? Was he just supposed to cover for us without having a clue as to why?"

Joseph simply looks on at us, afraid to speak.

"That's exactly what he was supposed to do. The less he knows the better," I answer.

"I disagree, what if we don't return in time? Did you want no one to know where we went?" Joshua asks.

"Yes, that's exactly what I wanted."

"But it's only Joseph, and he's only going to use the photo of the map to find us if they try and set sail before we arrive back."

"What photo?"

"My photo. The second copy, remember? We'll take yours, and I'll leave mine here just in case."

"You showed him the map?" I ask, my voice deep with disbelief. He wouldn't do this to me, not again.

"Of course, I did. He needs to understand it if something goes wrong."

I'm so angry I can barely think.

"You've told him everything," I say slowly.

"Now, Scarlet, don't be so upset. This is a dangerous thing we're doing, someone ought to know. I trust Joseph, and I think you do too if you're really honest with yourself."

But I've always had a streak of distrust with everyone I meet, some part of me that likes to keep most things from most people. Joshua was the first person in years I'd even tried to believe in, and adding Joseph is too much.

"It doesn't matter if I trust him or not, you've already decided I have to. Why don't I stay here and the two of you can run along and find the treasure together?"

"Don't be mean, Scarlet."

"Mean, I'm mean, am I? It's not *mean* to tell *our* secrets to someone else without even asking me?"

"It wasn't meant to be."

Joshua looks genuinely upset for what he's done.

"Perhaps, I overreacted," I say, after seeing how disheartened Joshua is. "It might be a good idea to have someone here who knows the whole story in case something happens and we're delayed."

"Truly?"

"Yes," and I mean it. "There's no one better to know our plans on this ship then Joseph."

Joseph releases a deep breath he'd been holding since I came back down the stairs. I may trust *him* with some of Joshua's convincing, but he is terribly afraid of *me*, and I admit, I do like it that way.

"And you won't be too upset if we give him a trifle or two of treasure?" Joshua asks, pushing his luck now that I've calmed down a bit.

"From your share, perhaps," I quip.

"Then feel free to tell everyone where Scarlet has gone, Joseph, clearly she doesn't mind."

"Fine, we'll give him something if we find something."

"Something descent?" Joshua checks.

"Decent enough."

"Never mind, Joseph, please keep our whereabouts to yourself pending a sudden departure of the crew."

"And even then, don't mention the treasure," I say, turning on him, "ever!"

Joseph can only nod.

"Relax, lad," Joshua says, as I head back up. "Just stick with the usual meals, and if anybody asks, tell them Scarlet and I are taking a walk."

"Right, Mr. Brisbain," Joseph states, smiling to himself as we climb up.

When we gain the shore, Joshua and I stay close to the shadows, trying to hide both ourselves and our belongings, creeping over to the tall trees and the thick vegetation that surround the area and sneaking away from the large group without getting caught.

Darkness washes over us soon after we push forward. No light shines down from above. The thick leaves and branches hover overhead making it nearly impossible for the sun to shine on the weedy and overgrown path.

Heading deep into the brush, the noises of the crew grow faint and distant, until they're non-existent. But the noises of true nature replace the sounds we've grown so accustomed to. A bird's flapping wings hit the leaves above, while the sudden croak of a frog shoots out from the left, and a constant trickle of water, we cannot see, hits upon rocks. A great difference from the creaking wood of the ship or the flapping of the sails.

I learned as much about navigation while on the ship as I could, though our honorable Captain never directly trained me. But I was ever vigilant and weary for a lesson he could unknowingly teach. And learning how to keep a straight path with the guide of a compass was just one of those lessons.

The Captain would sit at his desk and poor over his maps with compass in hand, while I cleaned the room, never seeming to notice I was there. Fortunately for me, the Captain mumbled to himself while working, and through those mumbled words I learned everything I could about compasses, maps, and how to use them both separately and together.

Even now, as we push through the jungle, leading us is easier than I expected. I hold the old and tattered compass Joshua brought with him in front of me. A four-pointed star, with each letter for North, South, West, and East in their appropriate spots, inlaid on the device. It may be well worn, but it is one of the most beautiful things I've ever seen. The glints of red and gold upon its surface only adding to its loveliness, as it rests in my palm. I don't think Joshua will be getting this back anytime soon.

"See, Scarlet. I knew I hadn't brought too much. And you were just complaining yesterday about my chemistry set," Joshua protests, as he struggles over a bush coming to his knee in height, and watching me as I work.

"I'm not using a chemistry set, Joshua. I'm using a compass, which is small and necessary and doesn't slide across the room about to shatter every time the boat rocks."

"That's not my point," Joshua continues, "I brought something we needed that you didn't want around. And we may very well use that chemistry set before long. You simply don't know."

"I know I don't like tripping over your things when they're scattered across the floor."

"You're impossible."

I hear Joshua's comment but refuse to answer. I have no desire to argue with him the entire journey about his excessive number of gizmos and gadgets. Instead, I focus on the compass and guide us south, following the directions of the photographed map.

The latch that keeps the compass closed is broken and slightly bent, but the compass itself is untarnished and shows our true direction. In our many months of sailing, I spent every night I could sneaking away to my old hiding spot, pulling the map from its secret place under the floor, and going over every detail, from the blue waves etched around the boarder, to the deep green bushes covering the middle of the island, but most importantly, memorizing the exact markings of the trail that leads to the treasure. Without these, Joshua and I could wander around the middle of the island forever without ever finding anything.

Confidently taking us deeper into the forest, I know I don't need to pull out the map every moment to verify anything. All is exactly as dictated. Every curve and every bush are perfectly matched to the curves and bushes promised to be here. The only difference is the size of the bushes, which have grown much bigger since the map was first written, and the visibility of the trail which has become more and more difficult to see with the passing years.

"Ouch!" Joshua suddenly says from behind me.

"What? What is it?" I turn to face Joshua, the kitchen knife I brought drawn from my side and poised.

But looking back toward him, prepared to fend off the attacker, I find that Joshua is not only *not* in mortal danger, but that he has caught himself in a rather large spider web spread between two trees.

"Ouch!" Joshua whines again, tangling himself further into the sticky webbing.

"It's only a spider's web," I say in annoyance, not knowing how he could have possibly got himself into such a mess.

"I know what it is, but it's tripping me up. I've stubbed my big toe twice now, thank you, and I would very much like to be set free if you don't mind."

I make my way back to Joshua, stomping down leaves and twigs in my return, the blade still out and ready to cut Joshua free. It may not be the grand heroics I thought I'd be performing, but at least I thought to bring some kind of weapon.

"You're not going to use that are you?" Joshua asks wide-eyed.

"Yes, lad. There's nothing else to use," I answer.

"But I..."

I don't wait for him to finish. I raise the knife high and slice downward, cutting the web away from the tree on the right side, and repeating the motion on the left, until Joshua is no longer attached between them.

"Wonderful, and how do you propose to release me from the webs themselves?" Joshua asks, his body covered in the sticky substance like a mummy with its head sticking out.

"I don't," I say.

"You 'don't'? You don't what?"

"Propose anything."

"So you're going to leave me like this?"

"Yes...at least until we think of a way to get you out without slicing you in half."

"Unbelievable."

Though he may not believe it, Joshua is forced to scuttle along after me in his web-dress until one of us can find a solution.

I can feel his dagger eyes on me as I walk and he hobbles along, fuming with anger, itching to say something to me about how terrible I'm being. I hear him open and close his mouth several times, without saying a word. He slows down and is about to stop in protest, when I hear a tiny noise come drifting in through the trees a little way ahead. I've finally found the small stream we've been hearing, and walk ahead to find it twisting between numerous tree trunks, cool and clear. Retrieving Joshua, I help him to climb inside the clean water. Though it is not very deep or very wide, it is enough for Joshua to wet the webs and dissolve them away. When he's finally free, he washes himself as thoroughly as possible from the grimy mess the webs left behind on his clothes and body.

"Disgusting!" he remarks.

"Try to stay out of the webs from now on would you, lad?" I say

"Try to stay out of...? I certainly hope you don't think I climbed into that web voluntarily."

"I'm simply saying that you're wasting precious time wandering about. Just stay behind me and we'll be fine."

"I think I've had enough of you today, young lady," Joshua fumes. "I do not like being led around a forest, in near darkness, by someone who doesn't have the decency to warn her partner there are webs along the trail, and then has him bumbling along after her for over an hour completely wrapped inside of them."

"I didn't see the webs and you should know where we're going by now."

"How can I when you run off to study the photograph every spare moment we have? I've barely looked at it since we boarded the ship, not even my own copy, and I hardly understood it when I *could* find the time. And now I'm supposed to blindly follow you? You hardly know how that compass works. I'm sorry, Scarlet, but you're going to have to work on your communication skills if you expect to lead this little adventure."

"I..." I'm amazed. I had no idea I was treating Joshua so poorly, or how upset he was. I was only attempting to get us safely to the treasure. "I'm sorry, Joshua. I don't know what to say. I only wanted to move us along."

"I know, Scarlet. And I know how excited you are about finally being here and that you can't wait to find your treasure and prove that you were right and get your ship and everything else you desire! But I'm...somewhat, older, than you and I can't stumble aimlessly about. I need to know what's going on or I can't help."

"Very well then, let's start this again. Shall we?"

I tell Joshua about the trail and what path we need to keep. Joshua offering his help by suggesting various timeframes we can follow to get to the treasure and back to the ship before it is meant to leave. With his plan, we will be allowed to camp at night and still cover the required distances during the day, insuring we are timed efficiently.

Having a set schedule allows me to separate the map into various sections in my mind; each day requiring a different undertaking, some requiring more time than others, such as the larger hills or steep inclines. By separating the distances needed to be covered based on difficulty, I can determine which days require excessive amounts of quick walking and which days required slow and careful progress.

It is a rough draft of what we will need to do in order to complete our goal, but our teamwork allows for a plan to form and for the bickering to stop. For the time being anyhow.

We move forward a little more before the night grows late and the birds' chirping begins to stop. I want to keep pushing us, the hunger for success is potent, but I know we need our rest. Joshua looks like a rag doll when he comes up next to me, clearly exhausted, and sweating through his clothes. We will be able to cover much more ground during daylight, and a good night's sleep will greatly refresh our energies.

We only have blankets to lie across on the hard, compact ground. After a bite to eat, we settle down across from each other to get as much sleep as we can.

Though still very warm, the night has chilled greatly, and we drift off to sleep quickly in the cool air, not even bothering to light a fire. But as soon as the morning comes and the sun begins to beat on the tops of the trees, the heat presses down with a sticky uncomfortable oppression and I can't sleep any longer.

I roll my blankets together before stuffing them inside my bag and grab a piece of food for breakfast. Finishing quickly, I see Joshua has barely begun to stir. Grabbing a second bite from my bag, I place the piece beside Joshua's sleeping face. The smell waking him more quickly than the sun's glaring beams. I smile, happy I placed it so close to his nose. With Joshua awake we'll soon be able to start off again.

By midday we spot a landmark and one of the symbols on the map. It is a single pine tree, over thirty feet tall, in the middle of a clearing. We'd both seen pine trees before, of course, there is nothing new about them; but never a pine tree that could grow in such humid conditions. The jungle is meant for leafy and lush plants, not spiky ones that usually live in cooler climates.

Our disbelief forces a reference to the photo, but it clearly shows a single pine tree in a round clearing. The map does not suggest any danger lurking in the area, and since we're now sure the photograph is not leading us astray, we look ahead to the next marker on the trail and begin to head southeast.

Bushes brush against our faces, wiping away the sweat on our skin with their silky surface. Our clothes hang wet and dirt covered, tangles of twigs knot inside our hair, as bugs we've never seen before, swarm in and out of sight and try to crawl in our ears and nose.

"I have eaten more bugs in the last hour," Joshua begins, "than I have eaten chickens' legs across my lifetime."

He blinks his eyes rapidly to keep any critters from making a permanent home inside his lids.

"This is genuinely revolting," he complains again, while trying to detach another lost soul from his tongue.

"I say this without cruelty," I answer, "but maybe we should stop talking."

"Yes, maybe, ugh, that was a big one," and he swallows it down hard.

Having eaten nearly every flying bug the jungle can afford, we finally come to a bug free area and are able to talk without fear of swallowing what few insects remain here.

But the lack of tiny, flying bugs does not mean an extinction to the species, and we're constantly surprised by how many there are in each place we trail through. Sometimes we come across colonies of ants or groups of bees, then find big, fat beetles slowly walking by, or monster sized spiders churning out webs for their prey. Both of us start to realize just how unpleasant the jungle can be in its natural state, when the wild spring free.

Our southeastern path soon takes a sharp turn west, when I spot a cave trying to hide behind a pile of bushes. I would never have noticed such a camouflaged and well-hidden place if not for the two lit torches on the outside of the caves entrance.

Chapter 10

"What do you suppose is in there?" Joshua asks, standing beside me. Both of us squatting down and out of sight.

"I don't know, lad, but we're about to find out."

After a few moments observing the cave, we approach cautiously, careful not to break any of the surrounding branches so we won't be heard, and slowly enter the cave. The light from the torches does not illuminate the inside very deeply, but I'm glad there is no light to reveal me and Joshua when I begin to hear low whispers not far ahead. It is of no language either of us have ever heard before, but it is still clear that whoever is inside is having an argument of some kind. Inching closer around the curved stone walls, we only stop when we see two men seated in the center of the cave, gently waving a handful of charms at a fire. They speak as they do so, but not to each other as Joshua and I had first expected. It is as if they are performing a ritual, a loud and angry one.

"We need to leave, now," I whisper to Joshua.

He's standing directly behind me, peering over my shoulder to see the two strange men. He cannot speak, shocked by the sight of the ceremony being performed in front of him, so he nods his head in agreement and begins to head back out of the cave as quietly as possible.

Hiding ourselves amongst the bushes nearby, we sit and wait for the men to leave the area. Not twenty minutes pass before both men emerge and we see them fully in the light of day. Tall, brown, and strong men, with long black hair hanging over their shirtless torsos. Hair so long it nearly reaches their grass skirts.

We wait until they seem a safe distance from the cave, before we climb out of the shrubs, grab the still lit torches from the outside, and re-enter the cave. Slowly we reach the area where the men had been shouting. The ground still strewn with remnants of plants left behind. A strong wind, filled with a foul odor, howls through the cavern and brushes our faces.

"What was that? Are you okay, Scarlet?" Joshua asks.

"Aye, I'm fine lad. But I'm not sure we should have come in here," I answer.

"What do you mean?"

"Do you believe in spooks, Mr. Brisbain?"

A second gust of air rolls in and extinguishes the light.

"Scarlet, please! Scarlet!" Joshua calls. "Where are you? I can't see you. The wind blew the torches out and I can't --."

"That was not the wind," says an unknown voice right behind him.

"Oh my," Joshua exclaims as he turns around.

When he does, he beholds the most hideous thing either of us has ever seen. It walks like a man, and talks like a man, but it looks nothing like a man. It moves with the wind, glowing in the dark with a white fluorescence, and never blinks.

"What are you and your friend doing here?" it asks, a heavy accent escaping its smoke-like features.

"My friend? So, you've seen her then?" Joshua asks as calmly as he can to this transparent man who floats in front of him without hindrance. "Where might she be exactly?"

"Right beside you," the stranger answers.

He points to Joshua's right side, and there I am, a hand held over my mouth by another spirit. I'm trying to scream. My neck red and tight from trying to push air through the translucent hand covering my face. But it does not matter, my screams are soundless, even a muffled cry cannot be heard.

"Unhand her, you fiend," Joshua demands, his strength increasing as he watches me gasping for air.

"No," the first ghost calmly replies, right before he grabs Joshua by the mouth and drags him off the floor.

Joshua kicks and screams, but his attempts are as fruitless as mine. The spirit is too strong and powerful. His cold transparent hands hold Joshua in place as he's dragged backward and deeper into the cave. Though he stomps his feet into the ground, trying to gain even the slightest advantage on his assailant, the ghost simply ignores his struggles, and tows Joshua along.

The spirit holding me follows his leader in the same instant, and they drag us deeper into the cold and dark stone walls. He has a harder time grasping me than the other ghost has with Joshua, but I still can't get free, and Joshua's kicking sends dirt into my eyes, blinding me as we push forward.

The trail leads us into another room, also made of stone and lit with its own torches, but this one has a stone slab placed directly in the center of the open space. Joshua's and my mouths are soon uncovered only to have our hands and feet bound with an invisible rope that lay against the flesh of our wrists and ankles like smoke, and though we know anyone could normally pass through simple smoke, this restraint is impenetrable. Some type of magic is binding us.

The spirits begin to speak to one another near the room's exit, but neither Joshua nor I understand what they say. It is the same language the two living men, who were in the cave earlier, had spoken.

"I demand to know what you lads are planning to do with us," I say, determined to gain some answers. Despite my fear, I have to try something to get me and Joshua out of this situation. "You see, we're on quite a strict schedule. Treasure hunting and all, and I was just trying to fit killing the two of you into the plans."

"There will be no treasure hunting for you," the leader of the two says. "And as for killing, that will be done by me."

The ghosts make their way back over and pick me up off the floor, placing me on the stone block.

"What do you think you're doing?" I ask, trying to wiggle free from their grip, but they remain silent as they lay me down and drift around the stone slab.

The leader leaves the round room and goes to another part of the cave, while the second spirit holds me against the cold surface of the stone. When the other comes back, he's brought a sword with him, a very big sword, with a white handle.

"A parting gift I hope," I remark.

The sword does not scare me as much as it does Joshua, who begins to weep in his little spot on the floor, completely bewildered by the rush of change that has suddenly come upon us. We've found ourselves so powerless so quickly. This was never on the map. There were no markings for ghosts or spirits. Our simple plan is already dashed, and we've only begun. Joshua begins with a new rush of tears, but I'm far too angry to cry. I should never have led us inside. My curiosity led us astray and now Joshua and I are going to die for it. I have to fix this somehow, but the spirit does not care about me or Joshua. His only care is killing each of us as quickly as possible, and for what purpose? Neither of us know.

He comes closer, raising the sword high above his head, aiming for my heart, as he begins to chant in a rhythmic pattern, words I cannot understand.

As the smoke-man reaches the highest point his arms can rise, he brings the sword down in a quick and accurate motion to kill. There is nothing I can do to stop him, and no plea from Joshua's begging lips can distract him. He is determined to slaughter me on the cold table until my heart stops pounding. No matter how angry I might be, I can do nothing but prepare for my coming fate, with a deep, hopeless gasp of a final breath.

The blade shines against the lit torches inside the cave, and I can see the reflection of the room in the shining metal. I can see the reflection of the two men who had been inside the cave earlier that morning, the two men who are running forward screaming at the spirits who have captured me and Joshua. All of this in the instant it would take the sword to swipe through the air and puncture my chest.

The noises of the two men catch the attention of the leader and he's infuriated. He turns away, and begins to attack the men instead. They do not move away from his assault. They've brought their charms with them and they calmly wave them back and forth while yelling at the two ghosts. The leader only wavers at their attempt, fading and returning, but his companion completely dissolves, like the smoke of a blown-out candle, and with him the bonds that hold Joshua and me in captivity, disappear.

Jumping off the slab the moment I'm free, I take the knife from my boot, come behind the spirit who had nearly killed me, and place the blade against his throat.

"No lad, I'm afraid I'll be doing the killing," I whisper in his ear.

"Ha! I think not," he scoffs. The two men who had stormed into the cave continue to chant, as I try to cut the throat of the evil spirit, but the knife passes through his smoky body without causing him harm.

"What? I don't understand," I say, loosening my grip on the ghost and staring at the knife in disbelief.

"The only thing that can kill me is this sword, and I am the one holding it. Not you." The ghost smiles at his own villainy and charges at me with the gleaming sword.

I jump to the left as the sword passes inches away from my arm. Out of instinct, I bring the knife in my hand up to block the next blow. Metal clinks against metal, the sword is stopped from crashing down onto the top of my head.

The blades are locked at the hilts. I push the knife against the blade as hard as I can and force the spirit backward until he smacks against the wall. Though he is uninjured, the sudden shift in power gives me the opening I need to rip the sword away from the ghost's hands. I twirl my knife around the hilt of the sword and give a heavy yank, sending the sword into the air and away from the spirit.

He is quick to realize what has happened and lunges for the sword before it's even begun to tumble to the ground. But the sword is already heading directly for the spot where Joshua is crouched down in his attempt to stay clear of the fight.

Seeing the sword coming toward him, he rises and reaches out his hand, and shuts his eyes, as the hilt falls into his open palm. The sword is heavy, but Joshua does not lose his grip, and the spirit can do nothing but stare, as the blade of the sword touches his neck in his rush to leap after it, and Joshua brings the sword straight through, cutting the ghost's head clear off.

The spirit dissolves into a puff of smoke, blowing out the torches, and leaving me, Joshua, and our rescuers in complete darkness.

Chapter 11

Joshua and I find the exit to the cave by following the voices of the two men. As we come into the light of the sun, the men stare at Joshua, a complete look of awe on their faces.

When the two men speak, Joshua and I understand nothing they say. The only clear thing is their admiration for Joshua, as they come closer and closer to him, admiring everything about him, going in circles, touching his arms, his clothes, speaking to each other, and to us, but since Joshua does not speak their language, he can only nod and smile, while enjoying the attention.

The only word the pair continue to repeat is, "Manatini," followed by exaggerated hand gestures that seem to indicate that Manatini is the name of the ghost Joshua killed.

"It wasn't that impressive," I remark, arms crossed, bored with this display already.

Joshua's cheeks flush at my remark.

"It was nothing really," he says, hoping to calm down the men and stop me from staring at him any longer.

"No, it wasn't," I state, brows wrinkling together in confusion, looking back and forth between Joshua and the two men. "I'm the one who actually fought the Mana-Man."

"Now, Scarlet, we mustn't be petty," Joshua chastises.

"I'm not being petty. I threw the sword over to you."

"Scarlet!"

"Well, I did."

But the two men carry on, ignoring me and smothering Joshua. They each grab hold of one of his arms and gently drag him forward.

"What now?" I ask, slowly following along.

"How should I know?" Joshua says over his shoulder, still continuing forward with the strangers.

The men keep making grand gestures with their hands, trying to explain to Joshua what their words aren't getting across. They clearly wish to show him something important, so Joshua willingly goes with them to wherever they're attempting to lead.

"Where are you going?" I ask, falling behind, since no one seems to care if I'm following or not.

"It seems they wish to show me something," Joshua yells back, "praise my bravery in some way."

"Praise? For what? Standing in the way of me getting the sword for myself?"

"Now stop it, Scarlet!" Joshua remarks, all smiles. "If they want to celebrate me they can, and if you want the sword so badly, here, take it."

And Joshua shakes off one of the men long enough to shove the hilt of the sword into my hand when I come closer, before he's dragged onward.

Fuming, I follow the group from behind, but I won't deny how happy I am to finally have a sword of my own. It's a little heavier than I expected, but the steel blade is bright and silver in color, and the white hilt has grooves over its surface for a tight grip. Between each angled line are little carved symbols I've never seen before. Among the ones I don't understand, the image of an animal will suddenly pop up. It's easy to identify the little bird, or the stag and horse, and one even looks like a hare. But there are so many I'll never decipher.

Entranced by my newly acquired weapon, I fail to realize Joshua is moving quickly out of sight, and I sprint after him.

The trail the two men lead us on is very far off the trail of our map, and I can't help but worry we won't be able to find the correct path again if we don't turn back now.

"Will you relax, Scarlet," Joshua says. "I'm sure these men can bring us directly back to the cave without any problems, and we will start right where we left off. And besides, it's getting far too dark to be walking about anyway."

Though it is getting dark, my mind is not settled, even if Joshua is right about the trail being easily found again, I don't like the idea of these strangers knowing anything more about our journey than they already do.

The men say little else as we continue forward. Joshua tries to speak with me while following our guides, but I'm still steaming about the incident in the cave and only grunt out replies, until he eventually gives up.

The bushes suddenly begin to increase in number and size as we go deeper, and I have a difficult time seeing the bodies of the men walking ahead. Everywhere I turn is a haze of green. Pushing forward, unsure of the exact direction I should be taking, suddenly the bushes completely cease and I'm standing next to one of the men looking out at a completely plant free void.

"Welcome to our home," the man says by gesturing to the camp in front of us.

It looks like a small town, with huts arranged in a semi-circle and a large fire burning in the center. On the brink of the village, the natives are walking about doing various activities. A very large group is huddled around the fire pit preparing some kind of meat near the flames. They are all dressed similarly in various vegetation-based clothes, their hair long and black and free on both the men and the women, and their feet completely bare.

It all looks so simple and comfortable and pleasant. For all the advancements we may have in England, you never see anyone as content with their lot as these people seem to be. They may not have shoes, but there also isn't a cold stone floor beneath their feet. And though their homes are not grand, I doubt any of them are struggling to pay the rent.

We walk into the village, following closely behind the two men. As we walk past their homes and around the fire, many people have gathered to their doorways or stopped their tasks to look at us. We smile slightly as we continue on, but the simple exchange is not returned, and we suddenly feel very unwelcome in this unfamiliar place. Seeing a group of people like none we've ever seen before is intimidating, and the inability to speak with one another only adds to the fear. If these people choose to be unkind, Joshua and I won't be able to do anything about it. But it helps to remember we were invited by the men we still follow, and perhaps that is enough to console the strangers around us.

Stopping outside the hut that forms the center of the semi-circle, it appears we have arrived at our destination. Entering the smoke-filled room, I can't make out the details of the inside. We both cough, as our eyes begin to fill with water from the sting of the strong scents that fill our nostrils. Our guides immediately bow to the ground upon seeing a man who has risen up from an unseen chair in front of us.

In fear of potentially insulting this leader if we don't follow our guides' lead, both Joshua and I kneel on the ground and bend ourselves in half, trying to acknowledge the customs of our new surroundings.

The man grabs hold of each of our arms and releases us from our bow. One of the men from the cave approaches and seems to be explaining what happened between Joshua and the Manatini to his leader. Hearing the name repeatedly mentioned makes it clear that his destruction is a bigger deal than either of us first imagined. The leader's face is covered in delight and he grabs hold of Joshua and hugs him so quickly and so tightly, he's lifted from the ground and gasps for breath.

"You're welcome," is all Joshua can manage to wheeze out.

The two men and their—I suppose "king" is appropriate—speak together once Joshua's feet have found land. With many smiles and nods between everyone inside, we exit the smoky hut with our two companions and are escorted to another hut ten feet down on the right. We enter to find nothing in the way of furnishings, but, apparently, we are meant to stay here.

"Not exactly comfortable," I comment.

"No, I suppose not. But it is still a generous offer," Joshua replies.

We both assume we're meant to take the room for the night as a thank you for destroying Manatini.

"Aye, lad, it is generous," I say, in response. "If you like the outdoors and dirt floors and wearing grass all day, then yes, it is a wonderful place to stay. I could live here forever."

"Alright, Scarlet, no need to be snobbish about it. We lived on a ship for months without even taking a regular bath and you're going to make comments about a dirt floor? At least they *have* a steady floor, not one that rocks under your feet without stopping for even a moment every instant of every single day. I feel sick just thinking about it."

"Fine, Joshua, you're right. It is the most generous offer I've ever had in my life and if we weren't busy hunting for treasure it might be the greatest thing to ever happen to us. Are you happy?"

"Yes, very."

Flopping onto the ground, I'm finally able to take my boots off, a stream of sand pouring out of them. Normally I would care about pouring sand onto the floor, if I were back on the ship, I'd be the one to clean it up, but here it simply blends in with the rest of the scenery.

Though it is a small home, it is still a home, a safe place to lay one's head, and if I wasn't so tired and hungry and annoyed with Joshua's sudden fame, I'd be perfectly happy to find myself in this new place with nothing to worry about.

"I'm going to see if they have anything to eat," Joshua says, once I've slipped my boots back on. "Will you join me?"

"Aye, I'm starving."

Emerging from the doorway, we take a good look around. There isn't much to see in this small village. It's obvious it was built in the clearing because of the wonderful coverage provided by the trees, so thickly packed on all sides that the only way to know about the village is to live here. With such a natural fence surrounding them, they are completely protected from any attackers; a perfect location for the families that have settled here.

The people walk about carrying baskets of fruits and vegetables and other plant life, and head in the direction of the communal fire pit. The smell of roasting meat drifts over to me and Joshua as we stand there, breathing in the weighty smoke as it takes over the air.

"Mmm," Joshua noises.

"Mmm, mm-hmm," I reply. "I wonder what that is?"

"I don't know, pork perhaps?" Joshua guesses.

"Maybe."

"Let's find out, shall we?" Joshua asks, gleefully.

Walking over to the pit, we wiggle our way in front of a few tribesmen. When we reach the object creating the most wonderful scent either of us have ever come across in our lives, we discover it is indeed a pig being roasted over the open flames.

Our mouths water as we come closer, the scent all consuming.

"Do you think they eat like this every day?" Joshua asks.

"I'd imagine they only eat like this when ghosties named 'Manatini' are killed," I answer, this being the only time I've been happy Joshua killed anything at all.

"No, I saw them fiddling over here when we arrived. Perhaps they've just had a good catch today. Do you think they'll start soon?"

"They'd better, or you and I are going to be forced out of our new home for eating an entire pig without sharing."

We see the King exit his hut a few moments after we arrive, joining his people, and giving a grand speech before the dining begins. Once he's finished, everyone digs in and devours the food. The people do not care for plates and silverware and such, so Joshua and I are free to rip apart the wonderful foods placed in front of us and consume every piece we can without worry or embarrassment. Though many of the people near us giggle and stare as we fill our mouths with more and more food, we're both too hungry to care.

And if we were in need of a bath before we arrived, we most certainly need one now to wash away the juices running unhindered down our chins. Joshua is nearly sick with eating so much, that he decides to retire early, leaving me alone with the few people who have fallen asleep by the fire, or who have created their own small groups.

I'm not one who enjoys sitting alone, only being able to look at the different people who are scattered around, instead of communicating with them, so I rise from my spot on the floor and walk around the village. There are many torches outside of the huts, lighting the path in front of each doorway, but no sounds come from within the little homes. Everyone who is not still by the fire, fell asleep hours ago.

But walking around the village gets boring, and I return to the fire pit. By now, nearly every person has returned home to get some rest, except the King, who is still sitting in front of the flames.

"Beautiful night, no?" I call over, knowing full-well he won't answer, but I walk over to where he sits anyway.

He smiles broadly as though he understands, but I know better. This is a conversation of one, even if two people are present.

"Indeed, it is," I answer for him. The King still smiling, still nodding.

"So, Miss Scarlet, where does this journey you wish to take lead?" I continue.

"Hopefully, very, very far away," I answer myself.

"Very, *very* far away? Well, I hope that it is not too far or we may never see each other again," I state for the King.

I do not know how to respond to my own statement. The thought of not seeing these people again had not bothered me before now. I was really only here because Joshua had insisted.

"There is a saying here," I continue, when I don't answer myself, "'Though you travel far, you cannot leave yourself behind.'"

"That's very beautiful," I complement myself.

"Yes, but more than beautiful it is true, and I think this truth applies greatly to you."

"Why is that?" I ask myself, as the King smiles on.

"Because you wish to go so far, you must also wish to stay far. Far away from what is behind you."

I hate to admit it, but I know exactly what I mean. "I think you may be right," I answer.

We sit in silence for some time after this. The King gazing up at the stars, while I ponder what I said on his behalf. I don't know why I'm listening to myself through the man sitting next to me. He seems to know more about my plans than I meant to reveal.

"I think I understand what you're trying to tell me," I say a little while later.

The King nods in confirmation as though he's understood this rambling creature beside him perfectly.

"I am sure you do," I say for him again, looking at his smiling face as though he has all of my answers. "If I did not think you would listen," I continue for him, "I would not have said anything. My fear for you, Scarlet, is that you did not learn from your past the way you should have. You are too willing to forget and pretend your life did not occur, that only the future matters, but it is the past that makes us and the past that creates us."

"But the future *is* all that matters," I point out to myself, "The past is irrelevant to what will come. How can one look ahead if they are always looking behind?"

"I understand your reasoning," I answer my own question. "But remember this: without the core of its beginnings, a tree would be nothing but hollow."

"You are very wise," I state.

"Thank you," I acknowledge.

Without another word between us, the King rises from the floor and heads to his hut leaving me alone again.

Chapter 12

Despite staying up later than anyone else, I awake early the next morning. Anxious to start off, I peer outside, only to find a wonderful meal left by the front door from our generous new friends. Joshua and I eat heartily, never having tasted anything so good in all our lives. The fruit is sweet and the water is clean, and anything we don't recognize is new and exciting and delicious.

Once finished, we grab our few belongings, exiting the little hut to find the people of the village waiting for us outside. The children and women are together, nodding and waving, the men standing quietly by, smiling. Our short visit seems to have had a surprising effect upon them, and the fear Joshua and I had when we first arrived, is quickly replaced with a guilt for wanting to leave. It seems we were more welcome in this little town than either of us realized.

The two men from the cave stand away from the group, prepared to return us to our starting point. The King is also among the group that has gathered. He nods his goodbyes to me and Joshua. Despite our lack of communication, it seems we've all been understanding each other perfectly well the whole time and our stay was merely a 'thank you' for defeating Manatini.

Free to leave this new-found place, we join the two men, who've already started to wonder away from the camp back toward the trail, as the people behind us bid farewell in their native tongue, until we can no longer hear them.

The journey back to the cave feels much shorter than the journey away. Perhaps it was not knowing where we were going the day before that made the trip so long, or perhaps it is the fact that we're now back on the hunt for our treasure, that causes the time to fly away faster, but Joshua and I are both very happy to be returning to where we left off.

"Are you crying?" I ask Joshua, as the two men walk away, leaving us to begin our journey anew.

"No," Joshua sniffles. "Why would I cry just because we're leaving the only two people we really know on this island, to hunt for a treasure we aren't even sure is here? Don't be ridiculous, Scarlet." And he wipes his eyes on the back of his sleeve.

I smile at Joshua's tears. He really can make deep friendships with anyone, anywhere. I just hope he doesn't fall out of friendships as quickly, or I might find myself on my own.

We find the correct path very quickly, but not ten minutes into the trek, the trees and plants become thicker than they've ever been to this point. When I walk through a pile of bushes, I disappear from Joshua's sight, forcing him to call out my name frequently to keep from getting lost.

I even begin to depend on the compass completely as we continue south-east, but even with the device in my hands, I don't feel secure in our direction. Matters only become worse when we break through the last of the vegetation and nearly walk straight into a stone wall.

"Well now what?" Joshua asks, when he comes through behind me.

"We've come to a stop. I'll go a few feet either way and see if there's a path around it," I say, truly worried I've led us astray and wanting to compare the map against the compass without Joshua's glaring eyes upon me. If I've really gotten us lost, I need to find our way out before I scare Joshua unnecessarily.

Hidden a few feet out of sight, I check everything three times, but there is no doubt we've traveled the correct direction. The map just never warned us there would be a giant cliff in the middle of our path, so I return to Joshua with the verdict.

"There's no way around it that I can see, lad. We're going to have to climb it if we want to continue."

"Do you see this thing, Scarlet? There is no way I can climb that," Joshua states. "There must be another way. There has to be."

"You're welcome to look for yourself, but I found nothing. I can wait here for you."

Liking the idea and believing it certainly cannot hurt to have a glance around of his own, he walks along the wall's path, hoping perhaps I missed something, but, unfortunately, I haven't. There is absolutely no way around the giant mountain, and it could be for miles before it ever breaks at all. And even if we can find a way, we don't know how thick the rock is, or how long it will take to re-find the trail on the other side once we arrive.

So, Joshua returns in defeat and terror, for he knows our only real choice is to climb over the rock face. We strap everything we have tightly to our bodies and begin to climb the wall with only a rope tied around each other's waists for safety, both of us hoping if one falls off the other can keep them from dropping to their death.

The wall is only slightly angled, making it difficult to find holes and crevasses to put our hands and feet in. Joshua and I hug the wall in order to gain any type of grip on its surface. The rock smells salty and metallic. After a few hours, I lay my head to rest against its cold black surface. I cannot see Joshua, who climbs a few feet below, but I feel the tug of the rope around my waist as he moves further along.

Joshua has a harder time of it than I do; his belly bounces against the surface and pushes him away regularly, but, luckily for him, I've already cleared many of the holdings before he ever reaches them, allowing him to gain a much better grip as he climbs.

Our progress only lessons the higher up we go. My arms ache and my limbs are tired and when I catch a glimpse of Joshua below, he looks nearly faint, but being caught halfway to the top and halfway from the bottom, we have nowhere to go. Frozen in place, our hands and feet shoved as deeply into the small holes and ledges as possible, we cannot move. We cannot reach our canteens for even a drink of water, because we cannot let go of the surface for even a moment. We cannot sleep, or eat, or even sit down for a small break. We are just pressed against a giant rock, that does not care if we live or die.

The moon begins to show itself above the line of trees beside us and we can see its silver glow when we turn our heads to the left and press our faces against the stone wall. The moon brings with it the cool night air, our only comfort after the sweaty and hot climb we still endure.

I wish I could stay in this one place forever, never having to move a sore muscle again, but the longer we cling to the wall without moving, the tighter our muscles become, and the cramps that come with our immobility are even worse than the pains of continuing forward.

"Come, Joshua, we must move," I say, as loudly as I can through dry lips.

"But, Scarlet, I can't. My arms and my legs, they're like wooden planks. If I try to bend them, they'll just snap right out from under me. Please, Scarlet, let's stay here for the night, we can hold on for a few hours," Joshua pleads.

"No, Joshua, we can't. Our arms and legs are going numb and then we won't be able to control them at all, you understand? We'll fall straight down. Now come on. We're mostly there."

I start pulling myself further up, digging my fingers into the small holes above, the rope tightening around me as I tug on Joshua, forcing him to start following.

We climb the wall for two more hours, our hands, arms, and fingers shaking from the pain and from the sudden cold brought on by the night, until I finally spot a small gap on the right side. It is just out of reach, but I can get there if I work over to it very carefully.

Joshua does not notice what I'm doing from below, until he's finally at the same height as when I stopped climbing, and the pre-made holes normally found above him, cease.

"Scarlet?" he calls above, worry escaping his voice.

"Joshua," I call over; nearly causing him to fall with surprise at hearing me so close by. "There's a rather large hole to our right, lad. I'm trying to get in there now. Just stay at this level and we'll work our way over together."

"Alright," he answers, regaining his balance and steadying his heart.

I'm only inches away from the entrance, as Joshua makes his way closer to me. Climbing inside, I gingerly turn around, careful not to tangle or yank on the rope around me and Joshua.

It is only a small indentation in the surface of the rock, but big enough for me and Joshua to sit in comfortably. Once Joshua is safely inside, he collapses on the floor, feet still dangling outside, more exhausted than he has ever been in his life.

"And I thought the storm on the ship was the worst thing that could ever happen to us," he says.

"Aye lad, this is much worse," I reply.

A few moments pass in silence while we drink water and eat the few morsels we brought with us from the village.

"Do you think they've noticed we're missing?" Joshua asks.

"Who?"

"The crew of course."

"Aye, probably. Unless they're too drunk to notice. I saw Bill unloading the rum when we left."

"Really? Then they must be miserably drunk by now. There was a *load* of rum in the storage compartment. If they've gotten into that, we could be gone for months before they'd notice."

"You're probably right," I say, with a tired laugh.

But for now, my only concern is falling into a deep sleep, before we finish our climb tomorrow. I look over at Joshua, leaning on the opposite wall already snoring. He fell asleep moments after eating, a few crumbs sprinkle his chest. His legs are brought up close. I follow suit, leaning up against my own side of the cave, knees pushing against Joshua's, and fall right to sleep.

The wind screams through the night, becoming worse as the hour grows late. The trees are rustling and the leaves are flying, and in the cave, the wind whistles against the walls like a terrible song. It starts off very soft and quiet and lovely, and then suddenly becomes very loud and menacing, and every so often, a high-pitched shriek vibrates off the cave's walls, jolting me awake. I have to grab the edge of the mouth of the cave tightly to keep from falling out, but Joshua keeps sleeping quietly away. Eventually it becomes too much and I can't go back to sleep, no matter how hard I try.

At first, I sit, looking up at the ceiling, counting the cracks the moon reveals, but this is not an adequate distraction from the cold wind that whips against my body and sends shivers through my limbs. Sitting up as much as possible in the little space, I decide to push deeper into the narrow cave, hoping it will be deep enough that the wind cannot get through and touch me and just maybe I can go back to sleep.

Crawling forward into the pitch dark, I travel only a few feet, before I reach the back of the small cave where the whistling actually becomes louder and higher pitched, like it's caught in its own echo and cannot stop. I lie down on the floor to see if the noise is any less shrill if my head is down. Though Joshua is still well within reach, the spot is already much warmer than the entrance. In this bent position, I brush my hand against the back wall to examine the surface, trying to find a little niche in the stone to curl up in, but instead of touching the surface, my hand vanishes before my eyes.

I jerk it back immediately in fear, thinking perhaps it is the lack of light playing tricks on me. If the moonlight cannot get through this dark place, then it must have only looked like my hand became invisible. Everything appears to be fine, the fingers wiggling freely without injury, I reach in again, and again my hand is completely gone. Reaching further in this time, too curious to be afraid, nearly my entire arm vanishes.

Bending further down, I try to see what exactly is dissolving my hand away, but it is far too dark to make out anything. Crawling forward even further, I find the darkness is actually a small hole, one so black I didn't even know it was there and can see nothing inside. It is nearly invisible itself. Feeling around the edges, I guess the size of the opening to be no bigger than three feet around, only just big enough to crawl through. My upper half tips into the hole, while feeling along the floor for any gaps I could fall into, before pushing myself back into the cave. What a curious thing to find in the middle of a cliff. And there doesn't seem to be any animal using the hole or the cave as a lair. I can't help but wonder if this is part of the map. The directions did lead straight on, as though the cliff wasn't there. Perhaps this is a precaution to keep the unknowing from finding their way to the treasure, and this was the true route all along. But just as likely, it is a natural cave in a natural wall that means nothing. I'm so preoccupied with my own thoughts, I don't even notice that Joshua has stopped snoring, and is now directly beside me.

"What are you doing?" he asks sleepily, when he sees me sitting there.

"Oh! You scared me. I thought you were asleep," I say. "I found another hole back here, but it's no use. I can't see a blessed thing."

"Another hole, really? Where do you think it might lead?"

"I was hoping it went straight through the rock so we wouldn't have to climb anymore."

"That would be fantastic."

"Aye, but it doesn't matter if we can't see where we're going."

"I might be able to fix that. I brought candle sticks with me."

"Of course, you did," I remark with a fake smile. "I should have known. You brought everything else."

I carefully crawl back to the entrance, while Joshua digs the candle sticks out from his bag. The candles are thick and red and Joshua places them in the candle stick holders he has also brought, handing one of them out to me.

"Great, lad," I say. "Now how do you suppose we light them?"

"I am glad you asked. I have been wanting to show you my newest invention for a while. I call it the 'twiglight.' I've been working on it since we boarded the ship, but I've only just got it to work," he says, as he takes another object from his sack. "You see, I take this little twig, that I have capped with a chemical compound, and strike it against any surface."

Joshua swipes the twig quickly across the floor of the cave. A spark shoots out of the head of the twig and is suddenly a small ball of fire.

"See, a 'twiglight.' And you said my chemistry equipment wouldn't be of any use."

Joshua brings the "twiglight" to his candlestick and lights the wick; he quickly does the same to mine and blows out the "twiglight" before it burns down to his fingers.

"That's the only problem," Joshua comments. "I can't seem to keep it lit for very long. It always burns all the way down, instead of staying at the top. But I guess that's to be expected when most of it is made of wood."

"Whatever it is made of, lad. You're a genius."

The candle's glow illuminates the entire cave, but most importantly the black hole we wish to climb into. It looks very much like the entrance to the bigger cave we're now in, just a smaller version.

Approaching, we shine the candles light inside. The walls are dark brown and cold to the touch. Even with the benefit of light, we can still see very little.

"Well, lad," I say. "I don't see an end to this tunnel, but if we don't use it, we have to climb the rock wall outside."

"I don't think I can do that, Scarlet. My arms are still like limp noodles after yesterday's climb."

"Alright then, I guess we have to try this path, and see where it leads us. Follow me."

I lay across the cave's floor, the candle in my right hand stretched out in front of me, while my left drags my body along. Balancing the candle is rather a difficult feat in such a tight space, but the small trouble it causes is well worth being able to see any dangers that lay ahead.

Joshua follows close behind, and squeezes himself into the tunnel's entrance. The flicker of both candles bounces around the cave's walls, and creates strange shadows of my and Joshua's bodies as we slide along the floor like snakes.

Traveling quickly at first, easily pulling ourselves along, our arms grow tired after what becomes many hours of dragging, and our legs will push us no further. We're forced to stop where we are and rest on the cold, dank floor. It is difficult to move in any direction in this small space, but Joshua manages to reach some of the food in his sack and splits it with me.

"Thank you, lad," I say. "So, what do you think?"

"About being here?" he asks.

"Aye."

"It's awful, but slightly better than climbing the wall. We could never have stopped like this. I was starving yesterday while

we hung there; just dreaming about the biscuits I had in my bag.
How much longer do you think it will take us to reach the end?"

"I don't know, lad, a few more hours I'd imagine."

"Good, I don't think I can stand much more than that.
My legs are already tingling and turning stiff."

Continuing on shortly afterwards, we progress steadily
forward, but our limbs give out again and we have to stop. My
neck is stiff from constantly lifting it to see in front, and Joshua's
shoulders ache from pulling himself along on his arms.
Eventually, we exhaust ourselves to a point where we can barely
move, and must call it quits for a short time.

"I thought you said a few hours?" Joshua accuses, as he
lights a fresh candle.

"It should have been," I explain. "We've covered more
distance in this tunnel than we would have ever faced on that rock
wall. I don't understand. We should be out by now, free, and on
the other side of the cliff face. I think we should go back,
Joshua."

"But, Scarlet, we've come so far. What if the exit is just around the corner and we don't even know it? It has to have an ending at some point."

"I suppose. But it could be blocked off," I say in fear.

"Well, let's keep going. Perhaps another day's journey is all it will take and then we'll be free of this wretched tunnel forever."

"Perhaps you're right. Let's get some sleep, a short nap to rest our bones, and we'll try again for one more day."

"Good, because to be honest, I really don't think I can turn around inside this thing. My bum is already brushing the ceiling."

* * *

We wake refreshed hours later, but the last of our candles have gone out while we slept, and being trapped in the pitch black destroys our positive moods a moment later.

"Perhaps we should have turned back. Why did we ever try this blasted tunnel to begin with?" Joshua says.

"Because neither of us could lift our arms above our heads," I state.

"Right. Well, perhaps we were a bit premature. I think we very well could have lifted our arms, or anything else for that matter, if pushed. We simply weren't motivated properly."

"And I suppose that's my fault?"

"Well, you are the Captain."

And so we went: crawling, taking small brakes, bickering, and then crawling some more. Again, for hours and hours, pulling ourselves forward until out of breath and out of hope. After a time, we just lay there not knowing what to do. There is no light, we can barely move, and we've seen no sky or trees or breathed fresh air for nearly two days. And try as we might to control ourselves, our food and water supply is running dangerously low.

"What if we turn back?" Joshua suggests.

"Even if we did," I begin, "we can't turn around because this place is too tight, which means we'd have to crawl backwards, and I can't see either of us moving quickly like that. So, it will take *at least* three days to get back to the hole where we started from, we would still have to climb the cliff face, and even if we get over the wall, we don't know what's on the other side. Not to mention we barely have enough water for today and only crumbs for food. We should keep going and hope we're closer then we think."

"And if not?" Joshua quietly asks.

I can only answer with the scrapping noise of my hands and feet as I slide forward across the rock floor. I don't need to answer Joshua's question, because we both already know the answer. If this tunnel doesn't end soon, we'll die right where we are, and no one will ever find us.

We move along in total darkness, feeling our way, not knowing when it will all be over. The noise of our moving feet is all that keeps the deeply dark hole from feeling completely deserted, but suddenly the noises stop.

"Scarlet? Scarlet, are you here?" Joshua calls.

The unexpected noise of my coughing comes back to him in response.

"Scarlet, are you alright?"

"Aye, lad. I'm fine. Come forward. I've got a small surprise for you."

Joshua is in more agony than he thought possible, it seems every event we encountered only added to his pains and sorrows, but the sound of my voice and the thought of even the smallest of hopes up ahead, spurs him forward.

My coughing continues as he gets closer to where I wait. It is still too dark to see much of each other's outline, but he can hear my breathing...above him.

"Stand up, lad," I say. "We've made it out of the hole—at least for now."

Joshua can hardly believe it's possible for him to rise from the dirty floor, but he sits on his knees without hitting his head, and continues to rise, until his shaky legs carry his entire weight.

He looks as though his limbs will give out from under him any moment, but he's determined to keep off the floor until they do.

"Oh! My poor back," he says.

He stretches his body and twists it every way it will bend, the sound of popping escaping from his bones.

"That feels much better."

"I'm glad," I say.

"What do you think this place is?"

"I don't know. Maybe just a break in the tunnel, but I've been feeling around the walls and there is only one way forward."

"Don't tell me it's through another cramped little space."

"No, lad, this path, cave, whatever it is, it keeps going for quite a while. I didn't want to leave you, so I'm not sure how long it will last, but for now we can walk through the tunnels instead of crawling through them."

"Oh, thank the heavens!"

"And better still, there's a small stream of water to the left."

"Where?" Joshua asks, unbelieving.

I take hold of his hand and place it inside the small pool.

"Another miracle!" Joshua practically cries, gulping handfuls of cool, sweet water, no one but he and I have ever tasted before. "If this spot wasn't engulfed in darkness, I would swear to never leave."

Too exhausted and scared to abandon the only comfort we've found in days; we don't head off right away. We finish our remaining food and drink our fill of water, stretching our legs and resting our muscles for as long as possible before starting off again.

The new path is not very wide, but standing up straight as we go through is more than enough to keep us happy. And the further we go, the less dark the tunnel becomes.

I noticed a change in the lighting a few hours into the trek, and the change continues to grow as we move along. Soon the walls are not invisible in the darkness, but instead carry a faint outline that soon changes into a clear presence. We not only feel the walls as we move, but now we can see every turn the tunnel makes before we reach it, eventually coming to a branch of the tunnel that forks off to the left and the right. But the path to the left is covered in rocks from a collapse years ago, making the right path our only choice.

"I just hope the only choice is the right choice," Joshua says beside me. "Get it, 'right choice' and 'right choice'?"

"Yes, Joshua, very funny," I answer, half-teasing, but Joshua continues to laugh at his own joke.

Since walking is so much easier than crawling, we cover much more ground much more quickly, and joy comes to us both when a lighted exit, a few yards ahead, reveals itself.

Blinded by the brightness, the strength of the glow stings, until our eyes are in tears. Walking out of the tunnel together, neither of us can see where we are or what we are standing on. The heat from the sun is scorching and the heavy air presses down, but it is a welcome change after the gritty dirt we've just left behind.

I blink away the tears and hold my hand to the level of my eyes, to block out some of the sun's rays. The sky is blue and a group of birds fly past. And directly beneath my and Joshua's feet is an enormous staircase, carved right into the other side of this great stone wall.

Chapter 13

"My word," Joshua says behind me. "Can you believe this? We've found stairs. Manmade stairs, carved into the earth. It's incredible."

"Aye, Joshua, it is."

Both spellbound at the sight, we pull the photographed map from my bag and examine the trail.

"Well, I don't know how we did it, Joshua, but that tunnel in the cave led us straight past the other obstacles shown on this map and directly to our destination."

"You're kidding?"

"No, lad. We're right where we need to be."

"I thought the tunnels might lead us past the cliff, maybe even off the trail a little ways, but I would never have guessed it was a shortcut—and a wretched one at that. Who would ever build such an uncomfortable path just to get to this place? It's completely ridiculous."

"I don't know, lad, but I'm glad they did. They must have wanted a second way to get in or out of here no one knew about but themselves."

"In case of emergency, perhaps."

"Perhaps."

But it was also possible, the cave was always the only way to get here, and the rest of the map was a lie to keep the treasure hidden from anyone who didn't know the secret. No matter how well we might have followed the map, if it led to nowhere, then we would have only ever been nowhere, with nothing to show for our troubles.

We would have failed if we hadn't been led to the little cave which brought us here.

With the sun rising on the left side of the stairs, we stand still, taking in our surroundings. Thick white clouds momentarily shade the skies, but when they disperse, the sun reveals a brick path at the base of the steps.

From the top of the stairs, our eyes follow the revealed route of the bricks as they form a snake-like curve through the floor of deep green grass and tall flourishing vegetation, before disappearing beneath an arch of trees.

"Shall we?" I ask.

"Are you sure this is the right way? That we aren't going into some kind of trap, or something? Perhaps it looks appealing because it's actually dangerous."

"No, Joshua, I'm sure this is the right way. Here, have a look yourself."

Taking the photographed map, he can clearly see this is the correct course. The map matches perfectly to the twisting, turning bricks before us, heading directly into the trees that are now so much bigger and more present than when the map was first drawn.

Carefully, we head down the weather-worn stairs, until our feet hit the landing. My boots tap against the stone, the noise bouncing off of the trees and increasing the volume.

"I do wish the scientists were here to see this," Joshua says, as he admires our surroundings. "They would be amazed at the many breed of tree we don't have back home. They grow so wildly here; I'm surprised they survive at all. And I believe I spy, a blueberry bush, just over there."

Surely enough, a fruit bearing bush lay just off the brick path. It's not a blueberry bush, but rather something native neither of us has ever seen before, but the fruit is sweet and refreshing all the same.

"The species of vegetation here is exquisite," Joshua comments.

"Aye, lad, the plants. We've walked on steps carved into a cliff and a brick road lain by men centuries ago, and you wish to admire the plants," I answer.

"I was merely wondering how they're able to survive here, that's all" Joshua answers in defense of himself.

I smirk at his frustration, laughing at the look he gives me in response, before returning my focus back to the trail. I'd noticed a bend some twenty feet back, a curve to twist the path further right, and now that we're coming closer to it, the end is only a short distance before us.

"Is that...?" Joshua asks behind me.

"Aye, lad, it is," I answer, with a smile.

Joshua realizing now what I already knew. Not only are we close to the end of the trail, but the trail ends at a solid gold door.

Approaching with held breath, because neither of us have seen so much gold in one place before, we look over the symbols carved around the frame of the door, elegant and fluid in their execution, like art through words, beautiful but, for us,

unreadable, and nothing like the symbols on the sword.

I quickly raise my arms to push the doors open.

"Wait a moment," Joshua says, placing a hand on my

shoulder to stop me. "Perhaps the words are a warning, to keep

us out of danger. Or worse, they're some kind of curse. What if

this place has a spell upon it? We could be cursed for the rest of

our lives, never able to live another day without the fear of magical

creatures hunting us down until they have killed us in our sleep."

Breaking out in a sweat at the very idea of a ghost stalking

him in the middle of the night, ready to suck the life out of his

body, Joshua's face goes pale, but I turn around to console him.

"This place is not cursed. There is no such thing as

curses."

"But..."

"No 'buts,' Joshua, if you want to stay here, go ahead, but

I'm going in, cursed or not. I'd rather have my treasure and hide

from spirits for the rest of my life then leave and wonder for forever what is behind this door. And besides, we still have the sword that killed that Manatini thing, so we should be fine."

Joshua takes a deep breath and looks at me hard.

"Your right," he says. "If we leave now it will have been for nothing. Let's go...even if a magical creature jumps out and kills us where we stand."

"That's the spirit!"

Reaching for the handle of the door, I gently turn the knob; Joshua holds his breath behind me, his eyes nearly shut. A loud squeak comes from the hinges, as the door, so long untouched, goes forward.

We're not surprised to see a room awaiting us on the other side, but we are surprised when the room is not submersed in total darkness. As the door swings in, we can clearly see the completely white walls and floor before us, the glow from inside pouring out, as we stare inside, both confused and slightly blinded. Stepping over the threshold, I reach out to touch the nearest wall, it feels like a pearl, and when Joshua's feet follow behind, they echo loudly against the floor.

The bright, white room is perfectly square, covered from floor to ceiling in a pearly coating, like the underside of an oyster shell, but the room itself...is empty.

"Is the door the treasure?" Joshua asks, slightly confused, "because I don't see how we're going to be bringing that back. I was under the impression there might be coins, perhaps some jewels, small things, things I could carry in my pocket."

But there is nothing Joshua thought would be here. We're in a cube of emptiness, brightly lit without a seeable source of light, no furniture to be had, and certainly no small treasures awaiting us. Stepping deeper into the room, a reflection glints across at us. There is a tall mirror on the back wall placed a foot above the ground and recessed into the paneling. The brightness of the room bounced so heavily off its surface, we didn't see the object when we entered, but moving about revealed the mirror from another angle, and we both realize it must be helping to spread the light source around the space, creating the intensity of whiteness surrounding us.

"How ingenious," Joshua comments, starring in awe.

I approach the mirror with caution, afraid that the floor may be rigged to fall beneath us if a wrong step is made. I do not believe in curses, but I do believe in the ability of men who want to keep the unwanted away from their belongings.

As I come closer, the floor holds sturdy underfoot and the mirror is no different from any other I've ever come across. My reflection looks back at me with the same puzzled expression I show it.

"What do you think it means?" Joshua asks, still halfway across the room. He has gone only a little further than the entrance, just enough to see the mirror from across the way. His fear of curses is still strong, despite his determination to cross the threshold.

"I don't know. It looks like a normal mirror to me," I answer, as I reach out my hand toward my own image.

My fingers brush my own fingers' reflection. It's cold to the touch, as my hand skids along the surface.

"Are you sure this is the right place?" Joshua asks.

"Aye," I answer quietly, entranced by the mirror as I stand before it, starring at myself, wondering if just maybe there is something more I simply cannot see.

"Well I don't see anything but that mirror," Joshua says, inching closer to it.

I stand back, raise my foot, kick the mirror in, and shatter it to the floor.

"Are you daft?" Joshua asks, instinctively covering his head to keep any flying glass from hurting him, despite his distance.

But as soon as the mirror is shattered away, the white brightness around us diminishes ten-fold, and on the other side of where the reflective surface once hung, is a dark stone room. Cold and damp, the smell of years of abandonment spring to life with my sudden disturbance. And scattered across its unkempt floor are thousands of pieces of treasure.

Joshua's mouth falls open at the sight of the riches before him, never has he seen so many pocket-sized treasures to be had. Excited and giddy, he begins to shout and dance around the white room, twirling his body with his arms spread out like wings. He looks so young and foolish, he's liable to hurt himself with joy.

"Now will you believe we're in the right place?" I ask, once he takes a pause from his twirling.

"I do, I do," he answers.

I rush into the room and begin digging through everything. There is so much gold I don't know how we will get it all back to the boat. Joshua finally comes in after his personal celebration is over and empties his bag of most of the gadgets and tools he brought with him, taking out three empty bags he had stuffed inside. He immediately begins filling them with various trinkets: gold, silver, precious jewels, all the while I stand close by, continuing to look around.

"It must be hidden," I whisper to myself.

Joshua stops filling his bags when he hears me speak.

"What?" he asks. "What must be hidden? It looks like it's all here to me. I certainly don't know what we would do with more. We won't be able to take all of this as it is."

"*Not the gold*," I accidentally snap.

I start walking around the treasure peering in every direction, under piles, between pieces, but it's all a different version of the same things, gold and jewels.

"I don't understand," Joshua says hesitantly. "I thought we were after treasure, and here it is, loads of it."

"Aye, loads, just the wrong load."

"Then what is it that you want, Scarlet?"

"The maps, they must be here, somewhere."

"What do you want maps for?"

"Treasure."

"Well now I'm completely confused. We have a map. We have a treasure. So, help me pack it all away so we can leave."

"*No*! Not yet. This must be a decoy."

"What is, Scarlet?"

"The treasure, it's all a decoy to distract us from the real treasure."

"You mean these things aren't real? It's all fool's gold?"

"No, lad, it's plenty real, that's the point. If we have real treasures, real gold and jewels, we'll think we've found everything, but we haven't. At least we shouldn't have."

"What else is there? The maps? What kind of maps?"

"Treasure maps, lad, more treasure maps leading to more treasure."

"All of this isn't enough?"

"Not for me, no. And it shouldn't be for you either."

But I truly don't understand. Yes, I certainly want the treasure, but what I need is something I heard about in stories as a little girl, and something I cannot seem to find. Perhaps I'm too late and it's already gone, but, no, this place hasn't been touched in so long, the story would never have survived if it had already been found. My parents would not have lied to me. The stories must be real, or this place wouldn't even exist.

"Scarlet, you look mad," Joshua comments, "please, explain yourself."

I look up at Joshua and see concern in his eyes. I hesitate to speak, I want to tell Joshua what I'm thinking, but I've held on to this story for so long, I'm not sure how to begin. Yet surely Joshua has earned my trust by now? If I can't tell him why I really wanted to come here, then there is no one I can confide in.

"When I was very small," I begin, taking a deep breath and focusing on the details I need to share with Joshua, "my parents would tell me the most fantastic stories about dangerous adventures and hidden treasures. But there was one story that I always begged to hear. It was the story of 'The map of maps.'

According to my father, many years ago, a village in the ancient lands of Ireland had gathered a collection of maps, and each of these maps represented a different part of the world where a treasure was hidden away from man. But the people who possessed them were extremely selfish and did not want the rest of the world to find the location of their many treasures, so they ran away to the southernmost tip of the world they could find, carrying all of their maps with them, and when they reached the uncharted place, they hid the maps so they could never be found by an outsider.

The villagers returned home once the task was complete, but they worried day and night that someone had followed them and stolen the maps away, pillaging their treasures from them while they slept. So, four men were chosen to return to the location of the hidden maps and to dedicate the remainder of their lives to keeping them safe from the rest of mankind, when those men left, they were never heard from again. Some of the villagers went back to the south to try and find the men, to encourage them and return word of their success in protecting the maps, but they could not be found. It seemed the four men took it upon themselves to find another location to hide the maps, a place not even their kinsmen were aware of.

Many years passed, until the son of one of the four men went searching for his father and found him hidden deep in the jungle. His father and the other men had built a sanctuary to keep the maps safe, and though the son tried to reassure his father that the maps were now safe and that he could return to his people, he would not listen and sent his son away.

But the son did not leave until he had drawn a secret map of his father's location. He returned to his people and hid the map away. But after many wars and battles between the neighboring people, the map was lost, never to be seen again. Many people searched for the map, knowing what vast treasures it would lead to, but none succeeded in finding it, not until you and I did when we broke into Mr. Everett's house."

"You're saying *we* found the lost map?" Joshua begins, clarifying the information for himself, as he processes everything I've just told him. "And we've followed it to here? And because that map was real the others must be as well?"

"Yes."

"And it only makes sense the maps are hidden in this place, because where else would they be?"

"Exactly," I almost yell in my excitement.

I knew I could trust Joshua. Yet again he's proven my instincts right. Thank the heavens above for bringing us together. Where would I be without such a dependable friend?

"But this is enough, Scarlet," Joshua states.

And my smile falls flat.

"This will allow me to build all of my inventions and then some," Joshua continues, "just like you promised. And I'm certain you could have any ship you've ever dreamed of now."

"But this is just a small piece," I say, beginning to pace with pent-up energy. "Surely you want more? More adventure, more travel, just...more."

"But I don't need all of that. And neither do you. Why are you suddenly so greedy?"

I stop walking around the room and turn toward Joshua.

"I'm not being greedy, lad. I'm after something— something bigger than the both of us."

Joshua is silent; he simply doesn't understand how important finding the other maps is.

"I don't know, Scarlet," he says after reflection. "It's not that I don't believe you, I'm just not sure that it matters."

"Those maps," I continue, "they lead to something beyond this little world. There is a place out there so grand that no man whose found it has ever come back, not a one. And its treasure is worth so much more than anything you see here."

"But I don't see any of your maps around, and I don't want to go somewhere no one's come back from, and I don't know why you'd want to go either? It sounds impossible, we could die. I've nearly died enough this week to last a lifetime."

"But it's not impossible, lad, not with your help. You know that machine you thought up? The one I asked you about back in England? The one all sketched out?"

"The submarine? Of course."

"That's what we need to find this place and get back safely. To succeed where no one else has. I didn't know if I would be able to do it on my own before I met you, but I know I can do it now if you'll help me. Won't you help me, Mr. Brisbain?"

"I...I'll try, Scarlet. You know I will, but I don't know why you want to do all of this..."

"Oh! Thank you, Joshua," I interrupt, with tears in my eyes.

"But I really must know what this is all about, the whole story Scarlet, not just the bits and pieces."

"Right, you're right, where to begin...there is a place somewhere in the middle of the ocean that no one seems capable of finding. Fleets of men have gone out to sea trying to find it, never to return, and no one can answer why, even the men sent to rescue the lost have been lost themselves. The only explanation anyone can give is that a creature must be protecting the area, sinking the ships before they reach their destination.

That's why I need you and your device. If we come to the place from under the water, instead of above like all the others, I think we can get past whatever it is that's taking everybody."

"Certainly, that makes sense, but how do you propose to find this place?"

"The maps that are supposed to be here, one of them leads to its exact location. All of the men who've found it before stumbled upon it somehow, probably following the men who'd gone before them, not really knowing what they were looking for, but if we can find its map, we'll know everything. Where it is, how large, which side is the safest to approach, maybe even what it is that's protecting the island and keeping anyone from returning."

"And you're sure the map is here somewhere?"

"Yes, along with a few others. The people who built this place didn't want anyone finding them. They're too important."

"Or too dangerous. Perhaps they had good reason for hiding them, Scarlet, maybe those maps shouldn't be found."

"But that was then, when they knew so little compared to us. Look how far we've come, look at your inventions alone, and certainly you can see how many things we once thought were impossible are now done every day."

"I suppose that's true, but I want you to know it will take time to build my machine, it's never been done before, and there will need to be tests, and re-tests, and..."

"Of course," I interrupt, "take all the time you need, well, not too much because we want to get there as soon as possible, but you take the time you need and get it done right. We wouldn't want to be stuck like everybody else that's tried, now would we?"

"No! Certainly not," Joshua says, uncertainly. "But we have to find the map first, correct?"

"Yes, yes," I say, slightly relieved.

"Maybe if we clear this treasure out of the room, we can find another door," he suggests.

"Yes, that might work. It's something to try at least."

I grab hold of the nearest trunk of gold and start pulling it toward the white room, so thankful to be doing anything. Joshua lifts a giant platter covered in various gems and follows me out. I cannot stop smiling, beaming with joy at revealing my secret to Joshua and having him agree to help me. The secret about the maps weighed on my mind as we crossed the ocean. Should I tell him? Trust wasn't the issue; it was his belief in the map's existence at all. Surely the fact we possessed one map should have been proof enough. But one map was simple, one treasure was possible. A hoard of other maps? Treasure beyond measure scattered across the globe? That might be asking too much of him.

I watch him moving along, as we push things about, and though, at first, he appeared willing and capable, there is a slowness coming into his movements, an unwillingness to continue working.

"Is something the matter?" I finally ask, afraid of the answer.

Joshua places the tray he has in his hands down before answering.

"Yes, Scarlet, I'm afraid there is, but I'm not sure how to say it. I don't want to upset you, but all of these new ideas of yours are bothering me deeply. I'm not delighted with this massive undertaking you're pushing us towards. A fear is starting to creep in, a fear that, perhaps, your being flippant about this whole thing. You seem to have completely forgotten about all of the difficulties we came into contact with just to get here. A dangerous sea voyage in unknown lands, an evil spirit who tried to kill us, and a tunnel where we nearly died of exhaustion and hunger and thirst, not to mention the steps taken to steal the map in the first place. I know all of that seems small now, with all this treasure real and surrounding us, but everything could have gone terribly wrong, we most certainly could have died more than once. What would treasure have even meant to two corpses no one would have ever found?

No, this was not the way I'd hoped things would turn out, and the prospect of a more dangerous adventure than the one we're still experiencing is not appealing in the least. You're going to have to create a foolproof plan before I will agree to build anything for any reason, no matter how many treasure maps we find along the way."

Disappointed by Joshua's words, I'm not really surprised. Joshua had no idea anything else was to be found, and asking even more of him is both unfair and unkind.

"I understand, Joshua, you don't need to help me any further. If the maps are here, I'll find them myself, and you and I can part once we return to England."

"I never said I wanted to part, in fact, quite the opposite. I have every intention of sailing with you on our ship and building all sorts of things, just like we discussed. I just want to be smart, and following a legend I've never even heard of before does not seem smart. I think, Scarlet, I'm just afraid."

"Me too."

"Really?"

"Of course."

"Then perhaps you have thought this through—not to say there isn't more to discuss, but everything about this is so new, and so unknown. It's more than I can handle at one time, more than I can wrap my thoughts around right now. I just need time to think and focus, but first we find the maps, see how true this story of yours really is, and if we find them, go from there. Maybe we can figure it all out as we go along, just like we have been."

"That's all I can ask."

"No, it's not, not with you." I smile at the truth, but we do regain focus and finish clearing the room before Joshua and I begin examining the empty space.

"It just looks like any other room, Scarlet. Four walls and a ceiling."

"That's what it's supposed to look like, Joshua, but the maps are hidden someplace in here, I know it."

Chapter 14

Joshua stands by the mirror entrance, while I walk around looking over different parts of each wall.

"Do you see anything?" he asks.

"No, not yet," I answer, annoyed. "You're welcome to join me, you know?"

Joshua walks over, after letting out a small sigh, and starts looking over one of the walls.

"What are we looking for exactly?" he asks.

"Anywhere in the stones that's different," I answer. "A different color, turned differently, even sticking out of the wall, that sort of thing."

"So almost anything, really?"

I eye the back of Joshua's head, while he pushes on a few stones. At least he's helping, even if he would rather be stuffing his bags full of gold. I turn back to the spot I was working on and keep looking for anything abnormal.

"Nothing," Joshua says, an hour later. "Not one rock is in the wrong place, or turned strangely, or even slightly a different color, so now what?"

Upset, I don't know how to answer him, I truly believed it would be easier to find the trick to the door or passage or hidden compartment the maps were supposed to be in, but nothing on the walls reveals anything. They're all exactly the same and in perfect order.

"I don't know, lad, I just don't know," I say, sitting on the floor in defeat, my hands on my knees, eyes staring down at the floor.

"Well, I'll wait for you in the other room," Joshua says. "We still have a lot of packing to do. Good thing I brought extra sacks inside my bag. Let me know when you're ready to help."

Joshua climbs through the entrance and I can hear the sound of coins being picked up from a pile, a few falling through Joshua's hand, and hitting back down to the surface. Irritated Joshua has gone back to his task, for not caring about the maps as much as I do, I wiggle myself further into the floor, refusing to leave the room for as long as Joshua is packing. He seems more than relieved there are no maps to be found, and no submarines to be built. I wonder if he even looked for the maps at all.

Sulking for as long as I can, I lie down and look at all of the patterns on the ceiling, every line and crack in the stone, as it shoots through the rock. One in particular catches my attention, I notice it looks similar to a deformed dragon winding its way through the stones, and I follow the image from the tip of its tail to the top of its lumpy head and back down again.

Once finished examining the dragon, I move on to another part of the ceiling, trying to make out another creature in the broken rock.

I think I've found a rabbit, but the longer I look, the more the cracks appear to be a fox. There is also a bear, very round and furry, but a piece is missing in the image. It's white in one spot above the ear and ruins the bear's face entirely.

Getting up off the floor, I place myself directly under the discoloration. Knowing it must be a smudge, and not wanting to help Joshua in the least, I look around for something to stand on, so I can wipe away the mark and make it easier to see the bear, but since we've cleared everything out, there is nothing to use. Forced to walk into the other room if I want to find what I'm looking for, I huff and head out.

"Ready to help, are we?" Joshua asks, giddy and annoying as he ties off a bag when I walk by.

"No," I answer, and stomp over to a big, tall trunk. "Are you done with this one?"

"Yes, I think I got everything decent out of there."

"Good," I say, and pick it up and carry it awkwardly back into the other room.

Too curious to keep working after my strange behavior, Joshua follows me back to see what I'm planning. But if he thinks I'm explaining myself, he's wrong.

Placing the trunk directly beneath the image of the bear, I climb on top and reach my right hand out, rubbing at the white spot, but it refuses to come off.

"Do we have any water left?" I ask Joshua.

"No, we drank it all in the tunnel."

"A rag then?"

"From my bag when I emptied maybe. Wait here, I'll grab it."

Joshua comes back with the cloth and hands it over. Scrubbing at the spot, the smudge will not come off. Rubbing harder and harder, I finally pull some of the stone away, revealing more of the white surface.

"No!" I say, in awe as I keep scrubbing.

"What is it?"

"I think I found it."

"In the ceiling?"

"Aye, lad, and it makes sense, who would ever look in the ceiling for the answer?"

"Not me."

"Exactly. The only people who would look up here would be the men who placed it here."

I scrub frantically, trying to work the thick grit away. When no more will come off, I step off the trunk and stand beside Joshua. We both look up to see what's been revealed: a perfectly round white gem recessed into the ceiling.

"What do you think it is?" Joshua asks.

"I think it's a trigger of some kind."

"Do you think it's dangerous?"

"It could be."

I jump back onto the trunk, reaching with my hand to push on the button.

"Perhaps you should wait out there," I say, looking toward the outer room, my hand hovering over the gem, fingers nearly grazing its surface.

"Perhaps you're right," Joshua replies, and he scurries out.

Turning back, he watches from the mirror's opening, as I place my hand on the trigger and push it in. The sound of grinding stone comes from above and moves across the ceiling. Unseen knobs and wheels, moving behind the thick stone walls, fill the room with a mechanical racket.

Joshua hears a loud noise coming from behind him and quickly turns around to see the golden door closing on us.

"Scarlet, the door, our exit is blocking itself off," he frantically hollers. I'm still standing atop the trunk listening to the devices working above. "Push it again and stop the door from locking," Joshua orders.

I hesitate above the gem, wanting so badly to see what it will do in the end, but I know not being able to get out is more important. I push the trigger again, but it is stuck inside the ceiling, not having reset itself from being pushed the first time. No matter how hard I press, the trigger stays put.

I keep pressing the button repeatedly, hoping that it will suddenly start working, but my efforts are in vain.

"We have to get out of here, Joshua, run."

He does not wait for me to say more, and runs toward the door before it shuts completely. If he can get there in time, maybe he can somehow keep it open.

His fingers wrap around the edge of the door, and he pulls as hard as he can, but the door continues to shut itself.

"Just get out," I call directly behind him, almost to the door.

Joshua releases his grip and pushes his shoulder through the opening, but the space is too small for his body, even as he tries to wiggle through.

I get to the door and try to push Joshua out, but the door is closing so quickly that instead of getting out, I have to help Joshua get back in before he is crushed. His shoulder slides back inside and the lock clicks into the frame.

"Thank you, Scarlet," Joshua says, winded.

"Of course," I answer.

We slide to the floor, taking a deep breath.

"Now what?" Joshua asks.

But the device in the ceiling is still churning, the sounds are still loud, as the wheels turn for the first time in years, and a metal gate suddenly appears and begins to close off the mirror entrance to the treasure room from both the floor and the ceiling, like teeth coming together, refusing to let anything else through once they are closed.

I spring to my feet and leap toward the opening.

"But, Scarlet, there's no way out of that room," Joshua yells, "We should stay in here."

"The trigger's in there, Joshua. If we stay here, we can't reach it. If you're coming, lad, it better be now," I say, still running, looking at him over my shoulder.

Joshua looks back at the exit and then at me.

"All right...I'm coming."

I turn back toward the gate and dive in, rolling across the floor on the other side, while the jaws continue to slide into place.

Joshua rushes behind me, grabbing his bag as he comes across, throwing it into the opening before himself. The gate grows closer and closer toward itself, as Joshua lifts one leg at a time over the sharp teeth. His movements are painstakingly slow, and my eyes grow wide with his dainty attempt to get over the closing bars. With his first foot in, he sits on the small frame, leaning further into the room. When his second foot is inches from entering completely, I grab Joshua's arm and jerk him through, both of us crashing to the floor with the force of our weight as the gate bangs closed, locking us in.

"Thank you...again," Joshua says, puffing the words out.

The sound of the crashing gates reverberates loudly off the walls, the two of us covering our ears until the pulsation subsides, but the device controlling the doors is still spinning and turning behind the thick walls.

The noise is so loud and so near. It's clearly coming from inside the very room we've chosen to lock ourselves into. We look toward the ceiling first, hoping the stone trigger has reset itself, but it remains the same. Slowly rising from our fallen position, a light starts to shine through a small slit in the stone, three feet above the ground, against the back wall. A slab begins to lift itself into the wall, and a bright blue and purple glow pours out of a hidden compartment. A perfectly square hole is open before us, a cavity chiseled away and meant to keep the greatest treasure in the room safely tucked inside.

I come to a seated position in front of the slot, watching as the stone finishes lifting itself away, and reveals the secret partition, Joshua peering over my shoulder. In the middle of the stone cutaway lays a wooden box, rectangular in shape, and carved on every side with the image of an eight-pointed star.

"Is that it?" Joshua asks.

"Aye, lad, I think it is," I answer.

I reach my right hand into the hole and place it on top of the box, but suddenly I freeze.

"It's too easy," I say.

"What is?"

"This box was revealed far too easily."

"If you call trekking the jungle, breaking down a mirror, finding hidden triggers, and keeping ourselves from being crushed by closing doors easy, then, yes, this box was by far the easiest thing I've ever found in my life."

"I mean this box is the most valuable treasure here, there must be a trick to getting it out."

"That was finding the gem in the ceiling."

"A trick to taking the box, Joshua, from taking it out of this hole."

"You can't just pick it up?"

"I'm afraid if I do, that we won't ever be able to unlock the doors again, like they're connected somehow. If I take the box, then, perhaps, there is no way to open the doors. The Maps can't leave if the people who have them can't leave either."

"I see," Joshua says, in realization. "Is there a spring around the box anywhere? Or a latch or something like that?"

I gently take my hand off the box's lid and crane my head in every direction to get a clear view of each side.

"Aye, lad, on the bottom I think."

"Where? Let me see."

"Directly between the box and the stand it's placed on," I explain, as he looks, "See the free space between them?"

"Oh, yes," Joshua says. He's standing directly in front of the box, eye level with the trap that has been placed, studying the device. "It appears that you were right, Scarlet. The box is most certainly rigged to do something if it is moved prematurely."

"What do you think we should do then?"

"Leave."

"That's not what I meant," I snap.

"Well, I don't know, Scarlet."

"What if I lift it really fast?"

"Yes, why don't you try that, Scarlet. Just pick up the box really, really fast. That won't keep us locked in this room until we both die. No, that will be fine. At least you'll have your bloody maps. Who cares if we're both too dead to use them?"

"Alright, alright," I say, perturbed. "But I don't know how to get out now that all the doors are shut, anyway, and I'm not leaving without the maps. I just don't have a plan for everything yet."

"Maybe there's a way," Joshua says, a sudden idea coming to him, "I think I can get your box out of there."

"Really!? How?"

"We can use our things to replace the weight of the box on that stand."

"Switch them out?"

"Basically. I'll gently lift the box while you replace it with my duffle. I hadn't taken everything out earlier, so the weight of what's left might be enough."

"Brilliant! Do you think it will actually work?" I ask.

"I'll have to leave my trinkets behind, but I don't know what else to do, do you?"

"No, not even a little."

"Then the bag it is."

Joshua hands over his satchel filled with heavy gold pieces and the gizmos he hadn't wanted to part with. If it's simply a matter of pressure to keep the trigger down, then anything weighing more than what's already there should keep the plate in place.

"Ready?" he asks once his hands are positioned over the box.

"Aye, lad, I'm ready," I answer. "Be careful, please, that box is very old."

"I know, Scarlet, I'll be very careful."

Joshua places either hand on each side of the box and slowly slides it across the little stand it rests upon until it reveals the first sliver of metal plating beneath. I'm ready with the bag, waiting to do my part. I lift it to the height of the stand and start to lay it across the surface area Joshua's work reveals. He's nearly off the first quarter, when it suddenly shifts upward from the loss of weight I wasn't replacing quickly enough.

A loud grinding sound comes from behind us and when we look, we see a stone block coming down in front of the golden door. Gasping at the sight, I quickly push more weight down on the trigger. The stone slab goes back up and away from the door.

"Sorry, sorry," I stammer, "I was watching you too closely and not paying attention to my own bit."

"Well I guess we know what would have happened if we had simply taken the box off," Joshua comments.

"Aye, lad," I reply, slightly shamefaced.

Joshua continues to slide the box off a little at a time, while I counter the weight as quickly as possible. With the last glide of the box across the spring trap, the box is free. I release the bag once it's equally spaced across the surface, and when nothing bad, terrible, or deadly happens, we both exhale, releasing the breath we'd unknowingly been holding the entire time.

"I can't believe that worked," I cheer.

Joshua hands over the box and we hurriedly sit on the floor, away from the unfriendly trap, to take a look inside. Gently lifting the lid, in fear of there being yet another trap within the box, I smile down, as Joshua and I gaze at the treasure inside.

Four maps, rolled into tight scrolls, each tied with a different colored piece of twine, are the only items inside the little box.

"Amazing," Joshua says. "And these all lead to a different treasure?"

"A different treasure and all the different places to find them," I answer.

"And where to first, Captain Scarlet?"

I smile at Joshua's joke, but I like the sound of it.

"Let's see, shall we?" I ask. I grab hold of the top map, pulling the knot out of the orange twine, and unfurl the heavy parchment.

Chapter 15

The dusty, curled paper of the first map unrolls unwillingly in my hands, the time spent untouched is obvious from the small cracks and tears that come across the page as I handle the parchment. Looking over the map, the treasure appears to be held in the middle of Newfoundland, but I'm uncertain, never having been there myself, though Joshua does agree that it seems to be the right place.

The second map I unravel has red twine and leads to Portugal. It is a clear location, because the country's flag is at the top, a marking we both recognize. Joshua opens the third wrapped in blue twine, which leads to Bermuda, another island, but at least it is closer to England than the one we're in now.

Opening the last map, tide in green, we find Ireland, my

homeland, and Joshua perks up at the thought.

"You can show me around," Joshua says, delighted.

"Show *you* around, apparently I need to show myself

around. There's been a treasure in Ireland this entire time and

I've never found it. Lot of a pirate I am."

But even with these newly found maps I find myself still

discontent.

"It's not here," I say.

"What's not?" Joshua asks.

"The map I came for," I state simply.

"It's alright, Scarlet," Joshua says, with a gentle pat. "We

have many other maps here we can use. Just look at this one, it

leads to Portugal. I've always wanted to go to Portugal and now

we can see everything there is to see," he states, taking the map

and trying to get me as excited as he is.

"*No*," I state, stubbornly, "I need the one."

I go back to the wall, certain that it must contain the answer I'm looking for.

"It must be here, it must," I whisper.

But looking inside the hole again, I see nothing new, nothing to answer my desires, and I dare not move the bag leveling the weight of the trap for fear of keeping me and Joshua locked inside forever.

While I continue to examine the hole hopelessly, Joshua is still looking through all of the maps, determined to enjoy our new-found treasure, even if I won't.

He takes all of the maps out of the box and lays them across the floor.

"It's funny how they are all different sizes and colors, isn't it?" he asks me, as I completely ignore him.

Joshua's observation is true though. Each is made from a different type of paper, creating different shades and textures. And though they are all of a rectangular shape, Ireland's is very small, while Portugal's is rather large.

"Fine then," Joshua continues, "keep searching for whatever it is you're looking for. Don't worry about me. I'll just hunt for these treasures by myself...if we ever get out of here."

Finishing his examination of the Portuguese map, he turns his attention to the wooden box itself and its many carvings. He runs his fingers along the giant stars covering the lid and the sides of the box. The inside is plain, just the grain of the wood running from one side to the other, so Joshua turns the box upside down to see if there are any designs or markings on the bottom.

As he flips the box over, he hears a small sound. Something seems to still be inside, even though we've cleared the box of its possessions.

Flipping it back over to look again, the box remains empty.

"That was strange," Joshua says to himself.

"What was?" I ask, still searching hopelessly around the hole for a clue.

"Oh, nothing, I thought the box made a sound, but it was nothing."

"What sort of sound?"

"I don't know. A falling sound, I guess. Like when you toss a container with something still in it."

I stop searching and turn toward Joshua.

"It sounded like something was still in there?" I ask.

"Well, yes actually, but I checked. There's nothing."

"May I see the box?"

"I suppose," he answers.

But being ignored for so long has made him sour, and he doesn't want to give up the box I wouldn't even look at two minutes ago, so he meanly shoves it into my hands.

I ignore Joshua's attempt at being rude and open the lid to look inside, and just as Joshua said, there is nothing but the bottom of the box. I close the lid and turn it fully upside down, when a sudden shifting sound is made.

"See, that's what I heard," Joshua comments.

Continuing to hold the box upside down, looking at it with a hard, uncertain gaze, I open the lid, and two things falls to the floor.

The first is the piece of wood that had created the false bottom of the box, which fell out of place when the box was held upside down, and the other is an old and wrinkled piece of paper.

It is much older than the rest of the maps, so when I pick it up from the floor, I have to unroll the parchment with the utmost of care. The paper sticks to itself and releases the smell of mold as it's unwound. The map itself is round in shape and sprinkled with the image of waves.

"Is that it?" Joshua asks, looking at the map in my hands.

"Aye," I answer.

"Well, where does it lead to?"

"The middle of the Atlantic Ocean," I answer.

"But there are no islands in the middle of the Atlantic Ocean, Scarlet," he laughs.

"Not on the surface."

"Wait, I don't understand. If there are no islands, or even land for that matter, then where can we possible go?

"Under the sea, remember?" I state.

"Under the sea? You're talking about my submarine again. I thought you just wanted to avoid some seabeast, not find treasure in the actual ocean."

"I never said that."

"But how are we...what about...I don't understand anything about how this is going to work."

"That's why I'm here," I answer, determined Joshua won't ruin my good mood now that I have everything I came for.

"And you expect me to build something I dreamt up years ago? Well, you better just find yourself another way to get there, because it won't be through the likes of me," Joshua protests.

"How else are we going to be underwater for such a long time without the help of your contraption? Your design is the only thing I've ever come across that even has the potential to succeed," I state.

"Oh, no, Scarlet, we can't. I haven't even built the machine yet. I don't even know if it works."

"It will."

"What if it doesn't? I haven't even tested a prototype yet. We have to test it before we can use it," Joshua says.

"What for? If it goes underwater with air and comes back up when we're done, that's all it has to do."

"It will have to do a lot more than that if we don't want to die at the bottom of the sea."

"Joshua, calm down, lad, I have complete faith in you. I know you'll build the safest submarine ever created..."

"The only submarine ever created."

"...and we'll find our way to the bottom of the ocean floor and the location of this treasure without anyone dying to get it."

Joshua pouts after hearing my crazy idea. I clearly don't comprehend what building an invention of such a large size will require, or Joshua wouldn't look so ill right now. I know the parts alone will be difficult to retrieve; he'll probably end up building

most of them himself, and even if he does, perhaps my

expectations are too high. He would be happy to have the

submarine simply dip beneath the surface, just out of sight, but I

want the thing to travel to unknown depths and navigate the dark

waters, and maybe that's too much.

"Besides," I continue, ignoring his reaction, hoping he's

simply exaggerating, "we have to get out of this place before we

need to think about building anything."

I re-roll the map and start to look around the room we're

still locked in. Too happy at our success to keep worrying about

problems Joshua hasn't even encountered yet. Right now we need

to find a way out. We have our treasure, and I have my maps,

and I'll take the peace of mind that comes with finding both, so

long as we can find the trick to getting out of here. The guardians

of these maps would never have created a cage they could not

escape from themselves.

I look back up at the stone I pushed earlier to close the gate, still recessed inside the ceiling. But the sight of it sparks an idea.

"Maybe there's another," I say to myself. "Joshua, start looking across the ceiling for any kind of trigger and let me know if you find anything."

Joshua silently goes to the other side of the room to look at the ceiling. An hour passing with silence between us, both too distracted with our own thoughts to speak. Joshua heavily weighted with the burden of an idea he never thought he'd create, and me realizing I'm finely in possession of my long searched for maps.

If Joshua only knew how many pointless trails I'd followed to get here, to reach this place, he wouldn't be so sour about having to create a little submarine. He's an inventor after all, isn't it his job to make things no one else has thought up yet? I just gave him all the funding he could possibly need, and now he looks sick over the prospect. He's going to have to gain a stronger stomach if the idea of a submarine scares him. I don't know what I might need him to build next, and it may be a lot more complicated.

"Here, Scarlet," Joshua calls, gaining my attention. "I *think* it's something, anyway. Does that look like another gem to you?"

I come over and look at the spot Joshua is pointing at.

"Aye, lad," I answer. "I think you found it."

Joshua and I go to the empty trunk we used earlier and carry it over to the new spot. Climbing atop, I rub away the grimy dirt from the area Joshua found and there, beneath another caking of dry mud is another trigger, only this one is made of a black stone.

"Well, here it goes," I say to Joshua, and push the stone into the ceiling.

As the black gem recedes into the surface, I can see the white trigger push back out some four feet away, followed by the sound of churning and cranking coming through the ceiling.

Joshua stands by the exit before I've even gotten down from the trunk. As the teeth shaped gates lift themselves apart, he pushes himself through the opening. Once his entire body fits, he goes into the other room and quickly grabs the two bags he filled before being trapped in the treasure room.

I'm not far behind him, carrying the wooden box with all five maps, but by the time I reach my own bag, Joshua is waiting for the front door to finish opening.

"Wait, Joshua, aren't you going to help me with the rest of the treasure?"

"No, Scarlet, I have quiet enough right here, thank you. I'll wait for you outside."

He squeezes out the door before it's fully open and continues up the brick path until he's out of site, leaving me to finish the packing.

Going into the white room and grabbing the last empty bag Joshua left behind, I'm surprised at how much treasure we'll have to leave, with gold scattered across the floor and jewels everywhere. We really did make a mess.

I head to the gems first, knowing they can easily be hawked in any village, and fill it to the point of breaking. Filling my own bag halfway with gold coins, after dumping everything but the compass and a few essentials, I place the wooden box on top, and stuff my pockets with anything that catches my eye.

I take a last look around the room, regretting not being able to take all of the treasure we've found, but I would rather safely return with what I have then risk being caught with a hoard on the ship. I do not know how the crew, or our Captain, would respond to all this treasure if we were able to bring back more. And hiding what we do have is going to be hard enough.

I fling the two bags over my shoulders and walk toward the entrance. For a first adventure, I'm very proud of myself and Joshua. It was not an easy thing for us to get here, sifting through the jungle to find this place, and then having to un-trap ourselves from locked doors, but we succeeded when I was not certain we would.

Grabbing the handle of the heavy ancient door, I pull it closed behind me, it bangs against the frame under its own weight, but it remains unlocked, waiting for the next soul to find what is left behind.

* * *

I find Joshua outside, walking up the path toward the staircase, and I trot along quickly to catch up with him.

"Joshua, wait for me," I call.

"Why?" he asks. "I would think you had some brilliant plan to get yourself ahead of me. You could leap over my head and land on the top of the staircase before I even lift my foot to the first step."

"Why are you acting this way?"

"Because, Scarlet, you don't care about how difficult building a functioning and properly executed submarine will be.

It could take months, even years, for the prototype to work correctly."

"Oh!—Well, I suppose I don't know all the technical bits and such, but I know you can do it."

"Scarlet..."

"Now before you start arguing again, we have all the money we need, right?" I interrupt.

"I suppose..."

"And you have all the plans figured out, right?"

"Yes, but..."

"And we'll have loads of time when we set sail. It will take us months to get out to sea once we have our own ship. You have time. Too much time if you ask me. I'd be there right now if I could, but instead I'm going to lose my wits waiting around for the ship to reach its landing, and you'll be having all the fun with your contraptions and gadgets."

"You think so, Scarlet? —That we'll have time I mean?"

"Aye, lad, I think we will."

"I just don't want you to get your hopes too high, Scarlet. If the machine doesn't work, I don't want you to think that means we've failed, or worse, that you have to do something drastic to get the treasure."

"I will try to control myself," I say, while holding my hand to my heart in exaggeration. "You just take the time you need, no rush, and if it doesn't work, we'll come up with something else. No need for anything drastic. Not yet, anyhow."

"I'm glad, that takes at least one worry away."

I'm happy to ease Joshua's mind, but I'm not certain I told him the truth. I want to succeed so desperately I don't know if I can stop myself from doing something extreme if I have to, even if that means risking Joshua's friendship. And that desperation scares me. Maybe I want all of this too badly, maybe it's not worth what I might lose.

Reaching the top of the stairs, we peer closely at the tunnel that led us here, the tunnel we planned to re-enter to get back, but it was such a very narrow space to get through the first time, and now with treasure bags in tow we won't be able to fit through like before, which was already painstakingly uncomfortable.

"I'll try first, lad," I say, "Give me the biggest bag."

Approaching the entrance, I turn sideways to thin myself. My body goes in easily, but when I bring the bag in behind, the burden of the weight is already noticeable and I'm not even crawling on the ground yet. I push myself back out onto the landing.

"I don't think this is going to work. And it only gets smaller the further we go in."

"I agree," Joshua says. "And we still have to climb down the cliff face on the other side when we get out. Perhaps there's another way."

"I certainly hope so," I comment.

Joshua and I head back down the stairs and look around for a different path.

"If we head away from the bricks, and directly into the jungle, we may find another trail to follow," I say.

"If that's the only way," Joshua replies, "then let's get started. We don't want to be late to the ship when they set sail again."

Cutting through the jungle on the right side, knowing it will lead us in the general direction of where we started from, the bushes and vines are a tangled jumble. The further we go along, the more I have to lead the way, while simultaneously cutting down the vegetation that consumes us on every side, with my new sword.

We try to maintain a straight path, but neither of us are certain we truly are. The map is useless when not leading us to the treasure; even when we try to reverse the instructions, too many images of the surrounding area are missing to help decipher our exact location.

I bring the compass out a few times, but the darkness created by the overlapping trees makes seeing the needle almost impossible. I'm guessing, more than I'm certain of, where north truly is, but with nothing else to guide us, we continue on with as much determination as if we know exactly where we're going.

Four hours into the journey, the thicker plants begin to thin. I'm able to put my sword behind me and walk through the brush with little effort in keeping the branches and leaves from hitting me in the face.

The sound of water comes rushing through the trees and the smell of floating salt soaks into my nostrils. We're getting very close to the ocean and it sends a jolt of new energy into my and Joshua's bodies.

"If we can get to the beach, Joshua, we can follow the shore back to the ship," I say, as I quickly continue forward toward the sound of the waves.

"Exactly what I was thinking," Joshua replies. He's so excited with the idea of getting out of the wretched jungle, he runs out of breath, as he bounds forward to catch up.

But our excitement does not last long. A torrent of rain breaks from the far distant clouds and sends a surge of endless water, made worse by the openness of our new location. The ground quickly becomes a massive puddle of mud, and fog drifts in from every side.

"Scarlet, I can't see you," Joshua yells.

"I'm right in front of you, lad," I shout back.

"What? I can't hear you. The rain is monstrously loud."

"I'm right here."

"Scarlet? Scarlet?"

I don't bother to answer again, instead, I walk back toward him. Searching for his outline, I cannot see him, but he continues to call my name and the voice grows louder as I draw closer. When I see his silhouette and I'm certain he is directly in front of me, I bring both hands around him and hug him across the waist. Joshua gives a start when he feels me, but just as quickly realizes who it is.

"Thank heavens it's you, but Scarlet, I can barely see you," he shouts.

I laugh at his reaction, still holding tight, "I know, lad, don't yell. I can hear you just fine."

"Sorry!" he bellows, and I roll my eyes.

"I have a plan," I say, "I'm going to take this rope from my bag and tie it around both our waists, like when we were on the cliff. At least then we won't be able to lose each other in this storm. You'll feel me tied to you, and I'll feel you tied to me."

"Good, get your rope out, and I won't move from this spot so you will still be able to find me."

I release Joshua from my grasp and fish the rope from the bottom of one of the bags, trying not to drop any coins while I'm at it. As promised, Joshua stays right where he said he would, with his arms raised to his head, ready for me to tie the rope around his waist. When I'm certain the knot is secure enough to not lose Joshua, I tie the other end to myself.

"Alright, lad," I say above the rain, nearly yelling myself, "now all you have to do is follow behind me. You'll feel the rope tug on you, and all you have to do is follow in the path it leads."

"Okay, Scarlet, let's go so we can get away from this rain if at all possible. Perhaps there's a ledge or something to hide under until it passes."

The rain beats the top of each of our heads, as I walk forward through the un-seeable jungle in front of us. The mud is extremely slippery by this time, and my feet keep twisting under me, causing uncomfortable pain in both ankles. Joshua is not having much luck getting through the soggy ground either. I continuously hear him grunt or cry out or even yelp as we move along. By the end of our journey, I'm certain neither of us will be able to walk properly again.

I lift my mud-covered boot from the ground and take a large step forward until it lands firmly in place, but when I go to lift my other boot, the rope tied around my waist tightens and my feet are stuck.

The rope tightens again and I can feel it digging itself into my lower ribs while it squeezes the air out of my body. Slowly turning myself around until I'm able to look directly behind me, my efforts are in vein, for in one fell motion the rope tugs at my waist for the third time and my body crashes into the ground.

The earth beneath me has turned into a slide, and I fly across the floor. I can't see through the brown sludge that splashes across my face, as I soar across the surface. I can hear a faint scream in front of me and know it must be Joshua. Has a wild animal attacked him and dragged him away? Has another spirit come out of the jungle to kidnap us? My mind reels, as I continue being dragged uncontrollably through thick muck.

The rope digs deeper and deeper into my flesh. Though I tied it around the outside of my clothes, the material is useless against the strong pull, I can feel it burning my skin as it pulls tighter and tighter by the unseen force that's dragging me along. If I don't untie the rope soon, it will crush my life away.

Tugging on the knots and trying to loosen them does nothing; the rope has been pulled too tightly to unravel. I push my hands deep into the mud on either side, hoping to grab hold of something, but my hands merely squish through the mud like water.

I look for trees on both sides, but they shift so quickly from view I barely see one before it is out of sight again, yet I know grabbing one is probably the only thing that will stop me and Joshua from being dragged any further.

I flip myself over into a sitting position, while gliding along, lunging wildly for the first tree I can. My face whacks off the bark and cuts my chin as I'm ripped away. I hit my head on the ground from the force, but the mud helps to soften the blow, keeping me from losing consciousness.

I barely spy another tree up ahead on the right and lung again, this time rapping my arms around it so tightly the pull on my shoulders feels like my arms could be ripped from my body, but instead, I'm yanked away by the momentum.

The ground underneath suddenly changes from a slushy mud to a rocky and branchy sludge, and though my body is ripped over with the changing earth, I do begin to slow down, and though I still cannot stop, it is enough to see what my best chance at ending this wild ride might be.

The rocks rip into my backside with a cruel sharpness, every stone and twig finding a way to stab and cut my flesh. I dismiss the pain as best I can, to focus on the trees, the many trees that are coming my way. I reach for the first one and bounce off the trunk, the second is too slippery from the green moss covering it, though I try to grasp it anyway. The third whips by so quickly there's no time to react, as does the fourth and fifth. Though slower, I'm still not moving slow enough. Looking a few trees ahead, I see a thick trunk with knobby roots rising out of the ground. I reach both arms out toward it, my focus completely on the tree's wide and gnarly body, before lunging and grabbing hold. The rope pulls and tries to carry me away again, but I won't let go.

I slide down the trunk, down to the roots and twist my fingers around the knotted wood that rises above the surface.

The rope pulls again, but with less force. I can barely breath it's pulling so tightly around my stomach, and my grip on the roots turns my knuckles white, but I do not let go, I cannot let go.

The dragging finally stops, but the rope around my body sways slightly as I continue hugging the tree.

"Hello?" a voice calls from in front of me. "Can anybody hear me? Scarlet?"

"Joshua?" I call.

"Scarlet, is that you? I thought I'd lost you."

"Aye, lad, it's me. What happened?" I gasp, still barely able to breath from the tight rope, my fingers aching as they maintain their grip.

"I'd be happy to explain everything, Scarlet, but right now I find myself in a very dangerous predicament."

"What do you mean?"

"Well, at this moment I am dangling from the edge of a very deep cliff and I would very much like to come up, if you don't mind."

I'm stunned at his words, if I hadn't stopped our downfall, Joshua would have fallen to his death and brought me down with him.

But even though we're stopped, I still don't have a way of removing the rope from my waist, and if I simply cut it off, Joshua will continue to fall off the cliff into a deep and horrific pit that I can't imagine.

I need a new plan and quickly. My grip firmly on the tree's roots, I raise myself to a sitting position, pulling the rope up slightly with me, but with the motion the rope tightens around me again.

"I guess I'm going to be squished then," I say to myself.

I take as deep a breath as the rope will allow, trying to alleviate some of the pressure, but it doesn't work. Slowly raising my body, while still holding on to the tree's trunk, I work my way to a standing position by hugging onto the tree as I inch my way up. When I can stand, I walk around the tree in a half-circle, bringing the rope with me as I go.

Using the tree as leverage, I release my hold of the trunk and begin to tug the rope toward myself with both hands, slowly raising Joshua away from the edge.

"It's working, Scarlet," Joshua calls.

I can't answer or regard his remark. The rope is still crushing me, making it difficult to breathe, and speaking nearly impossible.

"I'm almost there, Scarlet. Yes, I can reach the edge. O, thank heavens!"

When I hear Joshua say that he is safe, and can climb up the cliff's edge on his own, I fall to my knees, the view in my eyes a swarming black, and I collapse.

* * *

"Oh, Scarlet!" Joshua says, sitting beside me on the ground, "There you are. Are you alright?"

"What happened?" I ask, jerking awake and taking a full breath of air, finding myself lying on the ground, a worried Joshua kneeling over me, and the rain finally stopping.

"I don't know. I climbed up the cliff and I thought you would be there at the top waiting for me, but when I got over you weren't around, so I followed the rope's trail and found you lying here unconscious. Your face was completely blue, Scarlet. I cut the rope off of you and you started to turn a shade pinker. I think it may have been suffocating you. I'm so sorry! It's all my fault.

We were walking through that terrible fog and I stepped on a slick and molded over piece of ground. I couldn't catch myself and then suddenly I was sliding down this muddy hill unable to stop. I must have brought you down with me. I didn't mean to, Scarlet. I just slipped, but I nearly killed us both."

"It's alright, lad. I know it was an accident. If you hadn't brought me down with you, I don't want to think about what would have happened to you."

Joshua shivers at the revelation, "Me either."

Insisting I rest for a little while after such a nasty fall, we sit on the stony ground, happy to be safe, if not comfortable. Even if I hadn't passed out, I would still be thankful for the rest, knowing my body was covered in scratches and bruises from being dragged across the rocky ground, as was Joshua's. Though he never tried to grab hold of as many trees as I had. It never occurred to him to lunge at a wooden log to stop from falling, so his injuries are less severe.

When the fog has cleared in front of us, we feel able to continue on. The path is still misty around our feet and ankles, but everything directly in front of our eyes is revealed. Since I can see Joshua safely following behind, the rope is tucked inside a bag, much to the relief of my sore ribs.

With the path easier to follow, we reach the ocean quickly and set up a small camp on the sandy shore. Lying back, looking up at the night sky, the glinting stars shine brightly in the deep darkness above us. They disappear behind the gray clouds that float by, with their pockets full of stormy weather, then reappear exactly where they were before.

It being so much colder on the beach than it had been in the jungle, Joshua and I build a fire for warmth. With the charring wood splintering and cracking in the sand pit where it burns into ash, the light from the flames warms mine and Joshua's faces as we huddle near the blaze.

I yawn widely, before lying down again, drifting off to sleep in a moment. Joshua follows my example a little while later, falling asleep on his own side of the fire, smiling at the warm flames that coax him into peaceful slumber.

Such a long journey fills us both with a heavy weight of exhaustion we cannot ignore. Each of us positive we could sleep our whole lives away, so long as the fire keeps burning and the sun stays in bed.

But like every day before and countless days to come, the sunshine from the earliest morning rays comes down to warm me and Joshua even more deeply than our simple fire was capable of.

It wakes us in the gentlest of ways, and we're all too happy to open our eyes and see what this new day will bring.

We may have finished our first map's quest, but there is so much more for us to find and discover. The only way to learn about all that awaits us, is to get out of our sandy beds and carry on.

The welcomed rest spurs us forward along the beach's coast toward the ship and the crew we left behind. It feels like a very long time since we've been on board, and we each worry what our absence might mean. Will we be in some kind of trouble for leaving? How many questions will be asked of us? Did the crew leave without us when we could not be found?

Though Joshua and I are happy to have succeeded in our treasure hunt, we're also very worried about what the price of our adventure might bring.

"At least we can live with the natives if we get left behind," Joshua says, after speaking with me about the many concerns on his mind.

"Don't remind me," I reply. "Living in a hot hut with you for the rest of my life. Exactly the kind of paradise I had in mind."

Joshua pouts a little in offense. "Like living with you will be such a breeze," he says under his breath.

"What was that?"

"Nothing."

After a few days pass, we come to the last arch of the beaches coast, and see the ship rise into view out of the shimmering waters, still anchored in the sea awaiting our return.

When we reach the crew, the scene is not much different from when we left. Every one of the men is passed out on the sand with a bottle of rum clutched between his fingers.

"Good heavens," Joshua exclaims. "Did they drink every drop while we were away?"

"Most likely," I answer, tiptoeing my way through the mass of bodies that snore or groan or drool on the floor.

"Disgusting!" Joshua says.

I smirk at the comment. I'm surprised they waited this long to bring out the rum. A group of men alone at sea is not the ideal environment for sobriety.

"What are you doing, Scarlet?" Joshua asks, gingerly following behind.

"Looking for the Captain," I state.

"Ah! That is an excellent idea. Perhaps *he* can deal with these ruffians all scattered about."

I find the Captain furthest away from the crew, seated at a table that had been brought from the ship, passed out with an empty glass in his hand.

"My word," Joshua says, as he comes up behind me. "Even the Captain? This is unbelievable. I would have thought at least *he* would be more responsible."

"The Captain? Hardly," I say.

"What shall we do then?"

"Join them."

"Excuse me?" Joshua asks, astounded.

"Not like that, lad, but it seems obvious to me that no one here has any clue we've been gone this whole time, so let's pretend we haven't. Let's find a spot and join our comrades in a pleasant rest on the beach."

"Oh, I see! If they don't know we left, and we don't say we left, then it's like we never left."

"Exactly," I answer.

"I don't understand," Joshua says, confused.

"But you just said...alright, alright. If they don't know we left, then they don't know about the treasure, and we don't have to worry about anybody stealing what they don't know about. We'll tuck it away in my old hiding spot, keep an eye out that no one sifts through the area, and when we get back to England, we leave without anyone being the wiser."

"Oh, now I *do* see! Brilliant! Yes, Scarlet, let's join our comrades in a relaxing lounge on the beach, shall we?"

"Aye, lad, let's."

After hiding our goods onboard, Joshua and I row back to the beach and find ourselves a comfortable spot near the base of a hill, covered in bright green trees, with a clear view of the ocean as the sun sets against the horizon, and the sound of splashing waves hits the dry sand. This is the perfect spot to wait for our journey home.

As we sit together, each thinking about what has happened to get here and what will happen when we get back, neither of us can wait to continue. We have started an adventure that will change the very foundation of our lives, and it is the most exhilarating experience either of us could ever have asked for.

"Where do you suppose Joseph is?" Joshua suddenly asks.

"Let's see," I say, scanning the beach covered in our comrades, "Right—there."

And sure enough, Joseph is passed out on the beach between two other men, snoring away.

"Well, I would never have guessed it," Joshua says, after seeing where I've directed his gaze, "He was supposed to be caring for the crew in our absence."

"He was. Where do you think they got the idea to drink all the rum?"

Fin

About the Author:

H. D. Olson lives in Colorado. Having earned a B.A. in English from UCCS many years ago, it seemed only right to do something productive with it.

If you enjoyed this book, and would like to be informed of its upcoming sequel, and other works by its author, then please join our mailing list at: hdolsonbooks@gmail.com.

You can also follow H. D. Olson on, Facebook, Instagram, or Twitter, @hdolsonbooks.

And always feel free to leave a review on Amazon.

Editing by freelancer and friend, Tera Eling.

Cover illustration by, Jacob Ady, at 80 Designs. If you have a project of your own you would like him to consider, send an email to jacobady@gmail.com.

Copyright © 2021 H. D. Olson
All rights reserved.

Made in the USA
Monee, IL
04 August 2021

74470819R00166